"Staying together here is explosive."

André's words were firm. "Are you willing to face what will surely happen?"

"What will happen?" Caroline was lost in the vortex of her own feelings, her senses aflame.

"I'm going to carry you up those stairs to my bedroom, close the door, throw you on the bed, and not let you out until tomorrow...."

She licked her suddenly dry lips. The thought of it terrified her. "But... what about Matt...?"

Already André was turning toward the door. "If it only happens once, it's up to you whether you tell him, but if we get a relationship of our own going then I'll explain to him how it is between us," he told her calmly.

Caroline blanched. She could just imagine her father's reaction to that!

Other titles by

CAROLE MORTIMER
IN HARLEQUIN PRESENTS

CAROLE MORTIMER

the tempestuous flame

Harlequin Books

TORONTO·LONDON·NEW YORK·AMSTERDAM
SYDNEY·HAMBURG·PARIS·STOCKHOLM

For J.

———————◆◆◆———————

Harlequin Presents edition published April 1980
ISBN 0-373-10352-2

Original hardcover edition published in 1979
by Mills & Boon Limited

CHAPTER ONE

'BUT why can't he find his own wife, Daddy?' Caroline burst out. 'And why pick on me at all?'

'Because I told him I would introduce you to him, that's why,' said her father firmly. 'Now don't start being difficult. I've asked him here for the weekend, and I want you to at least be polite to him. You'll like him, everyone does.'

'You mean most women do! And if they like him that much, *they* can marry him, because I'm certainly not going to!' She glared indignantly at the equally stubborn man sitting opposite her. Her father often had weird ideas, but this was definitely the weirdest. No one in their right mind could seriously expect her to consider this ridiculous scheme of his, *except* for her father, of course.

Matt Rayner sighed heavily, his mouth set in disapproving lines. 'For goodness' sake, Caroline, no one's suggesting you marry him—yet. All I'm asking is that you meet him and try to like him. I don't know why you have to make such a fuss about one little meeting.'

'Because I know you too well. I bet you've already booked the church and hired the cars. It's just not on, Daddy. I won't do it,' she told him adamantly, smoothing back her long blonde hair behind her ears. 'He can't be much of a man if he can't find his own wife.'

Matt looked at the rebellious look on his young daughter's face and knew he had pushed the subject of Greg Fortnum enough for one day. 'Greg is very much a man, but he's also a busy one and badly in need of a wife. All right,' he put up a silencing hand, 'I won't mention the subject any more—for the

moment. But he'll still be coming here for the weekend, and I *do* expect you to be polite to him.'

Caroline picked up her handbag in preparation for
leaving. 'Of course I would have been polite to him,
but why you suddenly have this feeling of friendliness
towards the man I have yet to work out. You've always
told me he's an arrogant, ruthless and sometimes cal-
lous man.'

'*Business* man,' Matt corrected. 'There's a difference.
Inside business Greg is all of those things, but outside
the boardroom he's——'

'Just the same,' finished Caroline. 'I'm not completely stupid, Daddy, I can read. And some of the
things I've read about that man just don't bear re-
peating. And you want me to marry such a man,' she
added with disgust, flouncing angrily to the door of
the lounge.

'I do not! I just think it would be a good idea for
you to——'

'And what can he possibly think of me?' she interrupted him again. 'I ask you! You probably made me
sound like a husband-hunter. And don't bother to deny
it, I know your sales talk too well to believe anything
else. You've given me the same rubbish about four
times in the last two years, so I can imagine what you
told Mr Fortnum. I can almost feel sorry for him!'

'Well, that's a start.'

'No! How many times do I have to tell you? Anyway, I'm going away this weekend, so you'll have to
entertain your guest on your own.'

'Caroline! You can't just go off like this. What can
I possibly do with Greg all weekend?' Matt ran a
frustrated hand through his prematurely grey hair.

'I'm sure you'll think of something,' she smiled
sweetly before letting herself out of their apartment.
Let him sort that one out for himself.

Life roared into the powerful engine of her low

sports car and she accelerated out of the courtyard of their apartment block. It literally was theirs—or at least, her father's—and they lived in the penthouse apartment. Caroline breathed a sigh of relief, feeling as if a heavy weight had just been lifted from her shoulders. She just couldn't believe her ears when her father had made that ridiculous proposal, and it *was* ridiculous. But then she should have guessed, he had been very reasonable when she had told him of the end of her friendship with Anthony. She should have realised he had another applicant in mind.

For the last two years, since she had left finishing school, her father had periodically presented respectable young men for her approval, and she had just managed to shake off the most recent contender for her father's money. But this latest development was something completely new. Greg Fortnum was anything but a youthful gold-digger.

As one of the most wealthy men in the world, he was much in demand himself, and nothing at all like the manageable young men her father had previously produced for her inspection. This was why she couldn't understand why her father was so adamant about the two of them meeting. From what she could gather, Greg Fortnum wasn't a 'yes-man', and wouldn't meekly agree to her father's wishes. So there must be another reason for his insistence. She only wished she knew what it was.

Another thing that puzzled her slightly was Greg Fortnum's agreement to the idea. Even if he looked like a monster she was sure that some women would still be interested in marrying him, if only for his money. But then he didn't look like a monster, at least, so she had heard. He was older than the crowd she usually went about with and so their paths had never crossed. But she knew he was constantly in the company of some of the most beautiful women in the world. In fact, the last she had heard of him he had been having a tempestuous affair with one of the rather more well-known actresses. So why didn't he marry *her* if he needed a wife so badly? Why indeed? Yet another question she had set to puzzle herself.

She smiled impudently at the taxi-driver as she overtook him, and received a cheery smile back. She hadn't been going away this weekend, but she would certainly make sure she did now. No one, not even her father, was going to browbeat her into marrying someone she didn't love.

Esther was already at the table when she arrived at the restaurant for their luncheon appointment. Esther was one of her oldest friends, the two of them having met at school and continued to keep in contact even after Caroline had gone to finishing school and Esther had married John, her sober lawyer husband. With Esther being such a lighthearted girl and never taking anything seriously, and John being the exact opposite, Caroline had often wondered at the success of their marriage—and it *was* very successful. The two of them were just as much in love now as they had been when they first married two years earlier, in fact, probably more so.

'Hi,' grinned Esther, her short black curls bouncing impishly as she spoke. 'What's wrong?'

Caroline never ceased to be amazed at how Esther could always discern her moods without her even having to say a word. Even though she didn't particularly feel like it she found herself smiling. 'Daddy!' Her voice was eloquent with meaning.

'Oh.' Esther had become accustomed to Caroline's constant upsets with her father. The trouble with the two of them was that they were too much alike, although Caroline didn't have that iron streak running through her character that made Matt Rayner so successful.

'Mm,' sighed Caroline, smiling gratefully at the waiter as he placed her sherry before her. 'Daddy has another prospective husband lined up for me. The only trouble is he's gone one step further this time. Do you know who he's chosen for me? Greg Fortnum!'

Esther gasped. Matt *had* gone one step further. Whatever had possessed him to try and marry a beautiful girl like Caroline to a rake like Greg Fortnum? That man's reputation with women was notorious. 'But why? Why doesn't he just let you choose your own husband?'

'Because he thinks they'll only be marrying me for my money—or in this case, his money. Not very flattering, is it?'

'But I still don't understand. Look at the last one he introduced you to—Anthony, is that right? Well he was certainly after your father's money.'

Caroline waited until the waiter had left with their order before answering. 'I know that, but so did Daddy. Anthony was the type of fortune-hunter Daddy could handle, the fact that I didn't like him made no difference. He's so terrified I'll meet someone who he can't control that he's decided if I must marry it shall be someone of his choosing. But Greg Fortnum!' she said the last with disgust, staring miserably down into her glass.

'Quite,' agreed Esther dryly. 'Although he doesn't fit the description you've just given me. Greg Fortnum sounds anything but manageable.'

'I know,' sighed Caroline. 'That's why I think there's more to this than just Greg Fortnum needing a wife. Goodness, if he needed a wife that badly he has only to say so and thousands of girls would jump at the chance.'

'Mm,' Esther said thoughtfully. 'But perhaps they aren't the type of wife he would want. He would need someone who was used to entertaining people, someone beautiful and versed in all the social graces. And you have to admit you're all of those things,' she pointed out.

'You're beginning to sound like Daddy. Doesn't love enter into his plans at all?'

'Obviously not.'

'I suppose he would expect me to meekly sit at home while he went out to see his mistress. Well, I don't want that type of marriage. I want—I want a marriage like yours.'

Esther laughed, a tinkling bell-like sound that caused many male heads to turn in their direction. The two of them were totally unconcerned about the admiring glances that had been directed towards them during the last fifteen minutes, being accustomed to causing a stir wherever they went, one being so darkly beautiful and the other so fair.

'Well, I'm pleased that you find my marriage a good example of married life, but even John and I argue at times. I think all married couples do. As for you sitting meekly at home while your husband goes out, I certainly can't see that happening. But you're not seriously thinking of marrying him, are you?' She couldn't help but sound surprised, knowing how stubborn Caroline could be when she set her mind on something.

'Certainly not! I've told Daddy that he can entertain Greg Fortnum on his own this weekend, and I also told him I was going away for a couple of days. I wasn't, but I think I may go down to the cottage for a while. Anything to avoid meeting that man.'

'Go to the cottage in this weather?' Esther referred to the rain outside. 'But, Caroline, it's probably freezing there this time of year. Why don't you come to us instead?'

Caroline shook her head, tucking into the steak she had ordered with unconcealed relish. She might have argued with her father, but it certainly hadn't robbed her of her appetite. 'No, I think it would be better if I got right away from town. Thanks for the offer, though. Mmm, this steak's good,' she took a sip of wine. 'The cottage will be all right once I get a fire going. I could stay for a couple of weeks if I wanted to.'

'I think you would be better to come to us. You know we love having you and perhaps we could ask Nick to make up a foursome. John and I found a lovely new restaurant the other day, we could try that out again.'

Nick was Esther's brother, and although Caroline liked him very much, to her he was just like the brother she had never had. She and Esther were like sisters anyway, and so it had been a natural progression. 'No, Esther, it's lovely of you to ask me, but I don't want to be near enough for Daddy to find me. You understand? You'll be the first person Daddy thinks of contacting when he starts looking for me.'

Esther nodded. 'I suppose so. But I think you're making a mistake. Would it do any harm for you to meet the man? That wouldn't commit you to anything, would it?'

'No, except it gives Daddy a certain amount of satisfaction I don't intend him to have. I think the best thing for me to do is stay out of the way until he forgets all about marriage and Greg Fortnum. And I can work at the cottage.' She thought with pleasure of the studio her father had converted for her from one of the bedrooms at the cottage. As there had only been three of them to start with she had thought it very generous of him—she knew how he loved his comforts. Not that he spent a lot of time at their cottage, making Caroline regard it as her personal property.

John arrived a few minutes later to take Esther shopping for the afternoon, and after a few minutes' chatter

Caroline excused herself. If she wanted to reach the cottage today she would have to leave soon. She walked gracefully out of the restaurant, a tall honey-blonde girl with the face of a perfect sculpture. It was this perfection that kept most of the men who weren't fortune-hunters away from her, *they* couldn't be kept away by anything.

She let herself quietly into the apartment, but a quick look around assured her that her father wasn't at home. It didn't take her long to pack the necessary clothing for a stay at the Cumbrian cottage, just a few pairs of trousers and some thick jumpers to keep out the cold. Esther was right, January wasn't really the ideal month to go to her retreat, but after her father's earlier determination she didn't want to be anywhere he could reach her easily. He could be very persuasive in the right mood, and she wasn't impervious to his charm. The cottage was the ideal place to go in the circumstances. Of course there was a telephone there, her father refused to go anywhere there wasn't one, but if she didn't answer it he wouldn't know she was there.

She left him a note saying she would call him during the next few days, but that she refused to come back until Greg Fortnum was well out of the picture. She gave a nod of satisfaction and picking up the hastily packed suitcase, walked to the door. It was at just that moment the telephone began to ring. Caroline looked at it irritably; should she answer it or shouldn't she? If it was her father she could always pretend to be Maggie, their housekeeper.

'Yes?' she enquired curtly, automatically reciting their telephone number.

'Good afternoon,' greeted a coolly clipped voice. 'I wish to speak to Mr Rayner. Is that possible?'

'I'm afraid not,' Caroline replied politely. What an attractive voice this man had, although it wasn't recognisable as anyone she knew. 'Mr Rayner isn't at home at the moment. Could I take a message?'

'Certainly. Could you ask him to ring me back? Greg Fortnum is the name, he'll know the number.'

Caroline stared with horror at the telephone, looking at it as if it had suddenly turned into a viper. Greg Fortnum! The last person she wanted to talk to!

'Hello?' he said sharply. 'Are you still there?'

'Yes—yes, I'm still here. Did you say Greg Fortnum?'

'I did,' he replied, obviously becoming impatient. 'Is anything wrong?'

She could almost have laughed at this question. Anything wrong? *Everything* was wrong! She was calmly talking to the man who had clinically suggested marrying her! But then he didn't know that he was actually talking to her, Caroline Rayner, he probably thought she was the maid. 'No, sir,' she answered demurely. 'I'll tell Mr Rayner you called.'

'Thank you.' The abrupt click at the other end of the telephone told her he had rung off.

Well! So that was the famous Greg Fortnum. A bit abrupt perhaps, but definitely an attractive voice, sort of sexy. In the right mood and setting it could probably be downright seductive. She wondered if the body fitted the voice—probably, if his reputation was anything to go by. But then she didn't want to marry a rake, no matter how attractive he was.

Determinedly she picked up her suitcase again and walked hurriedly out of the apartment before she changed her mind, she felt a burning sense of curiosity to meet the man at the other end of that telephone conversation. But what good would it do her? If he practised the charm on her that the voice pointed to him possessing she wouldn't stand a chance, and before she knew what was happening she would have found herself married to him. And she didn't intend marrying anyone just so they could have an accomplished hostess to grace their home. No, she wanted to be the most important thing in the life of the man she married, not just another asset.

It was already dark by the time she pulled the car up outside the cottage, and pulling open the double garage doors she parked the car inside out of the rain. She had stopped on the way for supplies, and taking these and her case she walked over to the cottage. The key to the door was under the mat as usual and letting herself in she instantly felt the coolness of the cottage. She rubbed her already cold hands together. Thank goodness there were some dry logs beside the fireplace, it wouldn't take long for her to warm the place up and then she could get herself some soup to warm her.

She brought the sheets down from upstairs to air them in front of the glowing fire. A good night's sleep and she would feel better. At the moment everything seemed creepy, and though not normally a nervous girl she wished she hadn't come here now.

Her bedroom was quite warm from the fire she had burning in the small fireplace, but still she couldn't sleep. She had been here on her own before, but usually it had been in the summer months when the nights were lighter. She shivered as she heard yet another strange noise outside.

It was no good, she would never get to sleep. She sat up suddenly. There was that noise again, and it sounded like a car door slamming. What was a car doing here? This was the only cottage in the area, which could only mean that whoever was in that car was coming here. Could it be burglars? But there was nothing here to steal. But they didn't know that!

She crept quietly out of bed, peeping out of the curtains to the driveway below. Sure enough, parked there was a strange car, its sleek lines clearly visible in the moonlight. Her attention was caught and held by the shadowy figure walking around the car and delving into the trunk. She ducked back behind the curtains as the sleek head looked up at the cottage. Had he seen her? She chanced another quick look between the curtains. The intruder seemed intent on the contents of the trunk again. Well, it was no good cowering here, the telephone was downstairs, she would have to try and call for help.

The stairs creaked noisily as she crept down their winding length. Funny, she had never noticed they did that before. She only hoped the man outside hadn't heard it too.

She was half way across the hallway to the telephone when the door was flung open and the light switched on. Caroline blinked dazedly at this sudden light, wrapping her almost transparent nightdress around her slender body. The man standing silhouetted in the doorway didn't look at all pleased to see her either; his tanned arrogant face was creased in disapproving lines.

Caroline felt herself bridling with anger even in the face of danger. Who was this man to look down his haughty nose at her as if *she* were the intruder? She pulled herself up to her full height, looking coldly at the stranger.

The man moved forward into the light, his black hair shining like a raven's wing, and the green eyes set like twin emeralds in his mahogany tanned face appraised her from head to toe. He was a tall man, well over six feet, and although he had a lean frame Caroline could see it was pure ripcord muscle. The trousers he wore clung to the length of his thighs, and the thick creamy sweater disguised none of the power beneath.

'Well?' he queried softly. 'The maid, I presume?'

Caroline glared angrily at his sardonic face, resenting his scrutiny. 'Certainly not!' she said coldly. 'Who are you?' He didn't look like a burglar, that was for sure.

He put down the case he had been carrying, casually taking out a gold cigarette case and lighting the cigarette he had extracted with a matching gold lighter. 'Who I am isn't really important. It's who you are that matters, although from the way you're acting I would say you're one of the snooty daughter's friends. Am I right?'

'Snooty daughter?' she repeated sharply. 'What snooty daughter?'

The man came even further into the room, closing the door and moving with a cat-like grace to stand before the now dying fire in the lounge. 'Matt's snooty daughter. Cynthia, Catherine, whatever her name is.'

'Oh,' Caroline said dully. Snooty? Was she really? 'Yes, I suppose you could call me a friend of hers. But who are you?'

He continued to smoke his cigarette, his eyes narrowed. 'Much as I like the sight of your near-naked body I think you should go put some more clothes on if we're to continue this conversation. It may not bother you to be seen like that, but I don't usually carry out conversations with half-naked females.'

'Really?' Caroline said tartly, resenting his criticism of her. 'You surprise me.'

Those green eyes mocked her. 'Only females of my own choice,' he amended. 'And you certainly aren't that.'

She gave him a flinty look before turning on her heel and marching furiously out of the room. What an insulting man! And who was he, he hadn't told her that yet. Obviously an acquaintance of her father's, but who, that was the question? And how dared he call her snooty when he didn't even know her right name! Cynthia or Catherine! What a cheek! Well, she certainly wasn't going to tell him who she was, not after that description of her.

When she came downstairs again five minutes later, dressed in levi's and a thick green sweater, it was to find a steaming mug of coffee waiting for her.

'Help yourself to sugar,' he invited, drinking his own coffee with obvious pleasure. He put down the half-empty mug. 'Now, would you mind telling me what you're doing here?'

'Would *I*?' she demanded. 'What about you?'

'I happen to have been given permission to come here,' he informed her haughtily. 'And you?'

'Isn't it obvious? My—my friend gave me permission to use this cottage too. It has a studio, you see.'

'A studio? What sort of studio?'

'The type you paint in,' she told him sarcastically.

'Oh, I see.' The contempt couldn't be missed in his voice and her resentment towards him grew.

'Who are you?' she asked angrily.

He showed his dislike of her tone by the faint lift of his arrogant eyebrows. 'My name is André—André Gregory.'

'André? You don't look French. It is French, isn't it?'

'Mmm. And I'm half French, on my mother's side. And your name?'

'Caroline ...' she hesitated. 'Caroline Rawlings.' Why had she lied? It would serve him right if he felt uncomfortable when she told him her name, although she had the feeling it wouldn't bother him one way or the other. He seemed equally unconcerned that they had both come to stay here on the same night. He was the type of man that would be in control whatever the situation. She looked up to find him also looking at her, his face becoming a shuttered mask under her questioning gaze.

'So, Miss Rawlings,' he drawled her name, 'it appears that we both have the intention of staying here for the night. I could of course be a gentleman and say that I'll leave, but as good manners have never been one of my finer attributes, I have no intention of doing any such thing. Of course I only have your word that you are a friend of Matt's daughter—you could be an intruder for all I know.'

'But so could you,' she pointed out reasonably.

'Hardly likely. I happen to know the name of the owner.'

She thought for a moment. 'But if I were an intruder I wouldn't know if that were his name anyway. I would have to take *your* word for that.'

Reluctantly he smiled, showing firm even white teeth between his well-shaped lips. 'I see your point. Okay, we'll accept that we both have permission to stay here. The trouble is what are we going to do about it?'

'*I'm* not going to do anything. I was here first, so I think you should be the one to leave.'

'Why should either of us leave?' André Gregory asked calmly. 'There are two bedrooms, aren't there? Surely in this permissive day and age you aren't afraid to share a cottage with a member of the opposite sex?'

His tone could only be described as taunting, and Caroline blushed. 'I don't happen to belong to the permissive society.' And she didn't, hard as the pressure from some of her friends had been. Most of the men in her set thought she was frigid, although that didn't stop them trying to get her to sleep with them. Daddy's money again, she thought dryly. She didn't seem to realise that she was beautiful enough for any man to find attractive, her elusiveness making her even more so.

'You surprise me. Especially as you're a friend of little Miss Rich Rayner.'

'I beg your pardon!' She glared at him crossly.

'You heard me. That little girl is no better than she

ought to be from what I've heard, and if you mix with the same crowd she does and are as innocent as you say you are I'll be very much surprised.'

She stood up, her bearing almost regal in her anger. 'It may surprise you to know this too, Mr Gregory, but whether you believe what I've told you isn't of paramount importance to me. As long as *I* have my self-respect that's all that matters to me.'

She saw grudging respect enter those deep green eyes before it was quickly veiled and replaced with a taunting smile. 'All right. So which bedroom do I use?'

'If you intend staying you'll have to use the one to the right at the top of the stairs—I'm in the one to the left, so you can't use that one.'

He grinned. 'I could—but I won't. So,' he stood up, 'I'll use the one to the right. I trust that meets with your approval?'

'Would it matter if it didn't?' she said resentfully.

'No, *your* approval isn't important to me,' he ran a tired hand through his thick vibrant hair. 'I hope your story stands up, young lady, because if it doesn't you'll be out of here so fast your feet won't touch the ground.'

Caroline's eyes sparkled angrily. 'And just how do you propose to ascertain whether I'm lying or not?'

André Gregory smiled mockingly. 'Have you never heard of the telephone? I presume you have no objection to my using it?'

She shrugged her shoulders, thinking how ridiculous all this was anyway. Why didn't she just tell him who she was and ask him to leave, instead of continuing this pointless deception? If he hadn't been so condescending about her she would have never started this in the first place. 'Who am I to object?' she answered his question.

'Quite,' he said dryly, picking up the case he had deposited on the floor on entering the cottage. 'Now I'll wish you a goodnight—or should I say good morning.'

Caroline looked amazed at his calmness. 'You surely aren't going to go on with this farce? Look, it isn't that late,' she said desperately. 'You could stay at a hotel, there's a small one in the village.'

'Then why don't you use it? Because I'm certainly not going to. For heaven's sake, girl,' he snapped suddenly, regarding her through half-closed eyes, 'I'm not proposing to share your bed, only the accommodation. Or is that what's upset you? The fact that I haven't made a move to get you into bed with me?'

She flushed with heated anger. 'Some women might find your outrageous behaviour fascinating, Mr Gregory, but I simply find it disgusting!' She flicked her head back haughtily, meeting head on the angry sparkle in the eyes of this man she had only known for an hour. An hour too long in her opinion! 'And as you insist on staying here you'll need some bed linen. I presume you have no idea where it is?'

André Gregory regarded her through narrowed eyes, lingering insolently on the soft curves of her young body as if assessing what lay beneath her warm clothing. She resisted an impulse to put up a shielding hand, and saw the cynical twist of his mouth deepen as though he had guessed her thoughts. 'You're right, I don't. But I'm sure if you leave me long enough I'll find it. After all, there can't be many places to keep bed linen in a place this size.'

'It happens to be in the bedroom I'm using,' she snapped. 'And I'm certainly not having you barging in there when you finally realise that's where it is.'

'Why not?' he returned softly. 'It might be fun.'

Caroline's mouth tightened. 'Not for me it wouldn't.' She stood up. 'Now if you would like to come upstairs, I'll show you your room, and then perhaps I can get some sleep.'

'I wouldn't count on it. I plan to have a shower before going to bed, I'm sticky from driving so long,' he explained.

'Are you usually this inconsiderate, or am I the exception?' she demanded tartly. 'You have already frightened me half to death by turning up here in the middle of the night, accused me of being an intruder, and now you propose to keep me awake even longer by having a shower. You really are the limit!' she finished with disgust.

'Miss Rawlings—if that really is your name,' he saw her blush and raised a mocking eyebrow, 'which I very much doubt,' he added dryly. 'You appeared to be anything but frightened when I arrived, furious is more the word I would choose. And I didn't accuse you of being an intruder, I merely said you *could* be, there is a slight difference,' he shrugged his broad shoulders. 'As for the shower, I have every intention of taking that with or without your approval. If it disturbs you, I'm sorry. But I'm going to take one, of that you can be assured.'

Caroline didn't bother to answer him, recognising an obstinacy such as her own. And she knew she wouldn't have given in either. She opened the door that led out to the stairs, conscious of his firm even tread behind her. The bedroom she showed him into was the one her father usually occupied on the rare occasions he came with her. It was blue and white in decor, the fitted carpet blue, with blue and white and small touches of black in the wallpaper.

André Gregory looked around him appreciatively, placing his case on the ottoman at the foot of the double bed that dominated the room. 'Very nice. Your friend must have good taste in furnishings, if of course she chose the decor.'

'Of course she did,' snapped Caroline, standing nervously just inside the doorway. 'She's very artistic.'

'Hence the studio?'

'Hence the studio,' she agreed. 'The bathroom is the room next to yours. I realise you're probably accustomed to having your own bathroom but as there only happens to be the one I'm afraid we'll have to share.'

'And if I choose to walk around naked?' he taunted.

'That's up to you, of course,' she said coldly. 'But I would prefer you to curb these instincts if possible. I'm afraid I'm not used to seeing strange men walking about without their clothing.'

'Only men you know, hmm?'

'Don't be crude! You're very insulting, Mr Gregory. If you would prefer it I'll put the statement another way, I'm not used to seeing *any* man without his clothing. Does that satisfy you?'

He grinned. 'The name is André, and as I have every intention of calling you Caroline I would suggest you use it. As for satisfying me, only the best does that, I'm afraid.'

Caroline hadn't missed the intimate undertones beneath his words, and she realised how precarious her position was as she stood just inside his bedroom. 'I'll— um—I'll just get the bed linen.'

'You do that,' he laughed, shedding his jacket and beginning to peel off his thick sweater.

She fled before he took off anything else, like his trousers. She sorted through the linen cupboard, collecting sheets and blankets, but taking her time over it. She had no desire to find him in the state he had earlier described, although she felt certain he wouldn't feel in the least embarrassed if she did.

She tapped lightly on his bedroom door but receiving no answer decided he must already be in the bathroom. His clothes were scattered on the bare mattress, and picking them up she folded them neatly and placed them on the bedroom chair. It didn't take her long to make up the bed and she was just putting the finishing touches to the bedspread when he came back into the room.

She turned around quickly as she heard the door open, her face apprehensive. But she needn't have worried, he was clothed quite adequately in a thick white towelling robe, his dark hair gleaming damply. Caroline stood up from her task, rubbing her hands nervously over her slim hips, and unconsciously drawing attention to herself. 'I've—er—I've made up your bed,' she told him needlessly.

The green eyes mocked her. 'I can see that. And as you can see, as a concession to your supposed modesty, I'm wearing this robe,' he threw the damp towel on to the chair on top of his clothes. 'Was there something else?'

'No—no, of course not.' She snatched the towel off the clothing. 'You'll ruin these doing that. I'll put the towel on the radiator in the bathroom to dry.'

'Thank you,' his voice taunted.

'Right. Well, I'll—I'll go to bed now. Goodnight,' and she hurriedly made her escape, conscious of his mocking laughter behind her.

She found it even more difficult to settle down to sleep with the knowledge that André Gregory was in the room opposite her own. She could hear him moving about and wondered what he could possibly be doing now. Strangely enough, although she resented his presence, she also felt comforted to know he was there. She must telephone her father in the morning and ask about this friend of his, and perhaps warn him to back up her story when André Gregory called him.

CHAPTER TWO

CAROLINE awoke to thin watery daylight filtering through her lemon curtains. She blinked rapidly. Whatever time was it? She glanced quickly at her wristwatch, jumping hurriedly out of bed as she saw it was already eight-thirty. If she didn't call her father within the next fifteen minutes he would have left for the office. She grabbed her housecoat off the back of the door and rushed out to the bathroom, only to find the door firmly locked against her.

She rattled the door handle frustratedly. 'Are you in there, Mr Gregory?' she demanded crossly.

'I would have thought that was obvious, *Miss Rawlings*. So if you wouldn't mind going back to your room until I've finished shaving?' his deep voice sounded from the other side of the door.

'I most certainly do mind! You've had more than your fair share of time in the bathroom, and I'm going to wait right here until you decide to vacate it,' she told him stubbornly.

'Okay, please yourself. But I think I should warn you that I didn't bother with the robe today. I didn't think it was necessary as you appeared to be fast asleep.'

Caroline blushed hotly, feeling herself forced to return to her room. He knew very well that she wouldn't wait here until he came out of the bathroom, naked. 'All right,' she admitted defeat. 'I'll just go downstairs and put the kettle on,' and telephone Daddy, she could have added, but didn't.

'Quite domesticated, aren't you,' he taunted.

She didn't deign to answer him, running quickly down the stairs, her housecoat flapping aside as she ran.

Thank heaven she would have this chance to speak to her father privately before that man came downstairs. The telephone rang five or six times and Caroline wondered if anyone was going to answer when suddenly the telephone was picked up and her home number related to her gruffly.

She held the telephone close against her ear. 'Daddy?' she whispered questioningly.

'Caroline?' he queried sharply. 'Is that you, Caroline?'

She chuckled softly. 'Well, I hope so,' she teased. 'Who else do you know who calls you Daddy?'

'Where are you?' he demanded without preamble. She could imagine the anger on his face, he hated to be thwarted, and she had certainly done that by running out on him and his guest.

Caroline hesitated. 'I'm—er—I'm at the cottage.'

'You're what!' he exploded. 'What the hell are you doing there on your own this time of year? You know you aren't strong enough to chop wood and carry in the coal, and it's damn freezing there now.'

'I didn't need to chop wood and carry in coal,' she told him calmly. 'there was some already in the cottage. But as it happens, I'm not here alone, I have a man here who can do all that for me.' She grinned wickedly to herself as she imagined his anger.

'You have a *what*! What are you doing there with a man? You've always told me that sort of thing wasn't your scene, and now you calmly announce to your own father that you're staying alone in a secluded cottage with a boy-friend!' he predictably lost his temper.

'Calm down, Daddy,' she chuckled. 'You misunderstood what I said, I didn't say he was a boy-friend, merely that he was a man.'

'Same thing,' he cut in. 'I will not allow——'

'Daddy! Will you let me finish. The man staying

here is called André Gregory, and he says he's a friend of yours'.'

'Gregory? André——? André! Oh God,' he sighed deeply. 'Did he arrive late last night?'

'So late it could almost have been this morning. But how did you know?'

'Because I told him he could use the cottage for as long as he liked. At the time I didn't realise you were going to walk out on me in a childish temper and take up residence. You'll have to come home, of course.'

'I will not! Why should I! This is my cottage, you've always said so. And I did not walk out on you in a childish temper,' she said with disgust. 'You forced me to leave by inviting *that man* to stay for the week-end.'

'Yes, well, as Greg couldn't make it you can come home now.'

'What do you mean he couldn't make it?' Caroline almost laughed. 'Do you mean to tell me that after all that sales talk you did on his behalf he didn't even bother to show up?' she couldn't hold back her laughter any longer. 'Oh, Daddy,' she chuckled, 'that's really funny!'

'Hmp. I'm glad you seem to think so. So now you'll come home?'

She shook her head, suddenly realising he couldn't see her. 'No, I'm not coming home. I came down to the cottage to stay for a while, and I intend doing just that. Do you have any objections?'

'Plenty,' he said impatiently. 'But I don't have the time to tell you all of them right now. I have to get to the office, but I'll call you from there, okay?'

'Okay,' she agreed. 'But, Daddy—if Mr Gregory picks up the telephone don't ask for your daughter, just ask for Caroline. All right?'

'Now listen to me, young lady, I don't know what's going on there, but I want you home here by the time

I return this evening,' she heard him mumbling to himself. 'Do you hear me, Caroline? I'm ordering you to
get yourself home. Understood?'

'I understand you,' she agreed calmly. 'But I'm not
going to do as you say. I have a perfect right to be here.'

'Must I remind you that the cottage belongs to me
and I have invited a friend of mine to make use of
the facilities there? And you're not one of them.'

'You're damn right I'm not! But if this man is a
friend of yours surely you trust him not to make a
move like that?'

'Caroline, you've met André, and you should have
realised by now that I wouldn't trust him with any
woman, let alone my own daughter. He has a very
potent effect on women, and although you profess to be
indifferent to his charm I know it wouldn't be long
before you succumbed like most other women do. Am
I right?'

'No, you're not,' she denied adamantly. 'I've yet to
meet the man who could affect me like that, and from
what I've seen of Mr Gregory he certainly isn't the man
to do it. He's egotistical, pompous, and——' she broke
off as she heard a chuckle from behind her and swing-
ing round she saw the man she had just been describ-
ing leaning casually against the door jamb watching
her. How long had he been standing there? The words
screamed into her brain as she clutched frantically at
her open housecoat.

André Gregory moved forward with a feline grace
she found unnerving, his mocking eyes never leaving
her face. 'Don't mind me, Miss Rawlings, you just
carry on with your conversation. So far I've found it
very enlightening.' He sat down opposite her, toasting
his bare feet before the crackling fire.

Strange, she hadn't noticed that the fire had been
lit when she came down. André Gregory must have
been downstairs before her and lit it.

'Caroline? Caroline!' her father's voice crackled angrily down the line. 'Caroline, what's going on there?'

'Well—er——' she hesitated, conscious of the man sitting in the room with her. 'I'm sorry your daughter isn't there, Mr Rayner, but I really would like to talk to Cynthia some time today. Could you ask her to call me back?'

'Cynthia? Mr Rayner——?' Her father's puzzlement sounded quite clearly down the telephone. 'What the hell is going on there now? Why are you—— Oh, I get it. André just walked in, right?'

'Right,' she agreed with relief. 'So if you could pass on the message to her I would be very grateful.'

'All right, I'll call you later and then we can sort this thing out.'

Caroline looked up as André Gregory came to stand beside her, his hand outstretched for the receiver. 'I would like a word with Matt if you don't mind.'

'Oh—oh yes, of course. Mr Gregory would like a few words with you, Mr Rayner.' She crossed her fingers behind her back in the hope that her father wouldn't give her away. She handed the receiver into that slim tanned hand, careful not to come into contact with him.

He looked at her pointedly. 'This is a private conversation,' he said bluntly.

Caroline's eyes sparkled angrily. 'I didn't notice that I received privacy while I was on the telephone. You made no secret of the fact that you were listening.'

'I didn't notice you asking me to leave,' he said patiently. 'Now would you mind?'

Put like that she had no other choice. She glared at him resentfully before doing as he asked, slamming the door loudly behind her. A quick look in the open doorway of his bedroom confirmed her suspicion that he hadn't made his bed, probably because he had no idea how to. She straightened the sheets before tidying the scattered blankets. He seemed to be a rough sleeper, all the bedclothes were pulled out and it took her quite a few minutes to get them in order again.

'As one of Matt's daughter's friends I wouldn't have thought you capable of doing anything as mundane as making beds, but I've been proved wrong, you've done it twice now,' remarked the cynical voice that was slowly beginning to annoy her.

'Well, as you don't seem to be capable ...' she trailed off, having successfully made her point.

'Oh, I'm capable.' He moved forward dangerously. 'Very capable, as I'm sure some of my—friends would confirm.'

'I'm not interested in your—in your *sex life*.' Caroline moved away from him. 'Now, if you'll excuse me?'

André Gregory moved back to his former position, effectively blocking off her exit. He looked down at her defiant chin, a slight grin on his rugged features. 'I didn't realise I was talking about my—sex life,' he paused as she had done, a purely mocking gesture, 'but since we're on the subject, just which one of the Rayner family are you a friend of?'

'What's that supposed to mean?' she demanded icily.

His eyes flickered over her contemptuously. 'What do you think I mean? Matt was singing your praises a few moments ago, with no mention of his daughter. Also he warned me off you, which in my estimation can only mean one thing. What I would like to know is what does the snooty daughter think of your friendship, if she knows about it, of course?'

Caroline couldn't believe what she was hearing. She stared at him in horror. 'How can you stand there and say something like that about a man you claim is a friend of yours? If—Mr Rayner has friends like you he certainly doesn't need any enemies!'

His smile deepened with sarcasm. 'Come on, girl! Matt may be a friend of mine, but he's also a man, with a man's appetites.' He studied her appraisingly. 'And you're not bad to look at.'

'Thanks for nothing!' she snapped, intending to sweep past him but finding herself held in a vice-like grip. 'Will you let go of my arm!'

His other hand came round to push up her chin, and it wasn't a gentle gesture. 'If I tell you that you're unusually beautiful, will you calm down?'

She pushed his hand away. 'No, I won't! You see, I'm not susceptible to charmers like you. And after all the insults you've directed at—Mr Rayner and myself, I don't see why I should bother to speak to you at all. Mr Rayner is a highly respected business man, and quite old enough to be my father.'

'So am I—just. If I had a very misspent youth— which I probably did. But my own feelings towards you are anything but fatherly. You aren't the type of girl to bring out those sort of instincts in a man—far from it. Especially dressed as you are now. Are you aware of the fact that on the two occasions we've met you've been dressed in a shimmering nightdress and a not very substantial wrap respectively, hardly the right attire to inspire mere friendship.'

'I don't happen to want your friendship,' Caroline told him haughtily. 'And as my clothing is so offensive to you I'll go and dress.'

'Oh, your clothing doesn't offend me, on the contrary, I find it very—stimulating. But as I've had the warning off signal from Matt I don't want to poach on another man's preserve.'

'I'm not any man's *preserve*,' she snapped angrily. 'Especially not Mr Rayner's. Now get out of my way!'

His hand tightened about her wrist and she winced with the pain. 'Naughty, naughty, Caroline. Now say you're sorry for being rude to me.'

'I will not! Why should I?'

He raised his eyes heavenward as if losing patience with her. 'Why indeed?' he humoured before his face hardened and his eyes became like glittering emeralds. 'Because I just said you should! One thing I cannot abide is rude little girls like yourself who should have had a few more beatings when they were younger, their parents leaving the task of taming them to the poor unsuspecting fool who marries them.'

'Do you speak from experience, Mr Gregory?'

He laughed harshly. 'Not exactly. I haven't yet been stupid enough to get caught in that trap. But I've seen enough of my friends' wives to know what I'm talking about.'

'I'm sure you have,' Caroline agreed bitchily. 'From close quarters, no doubt?'

'Very close quarters in some cases, but then I'm sure you'd already guessed that.' He released her hand, unbalancing her with the suddenness of the movement. Caroline reached out to stop herself falling, and found herself held rigidly against this man's warm body, his breath lightly fanning her hair.

She struggled in his arms. 'Let go of me,' she said through gritted teeth. 'Take your—your hands off me!'

André Gregory let her go immediately, pushing her casually away from him. 'I think I'm beginning to believe you when you say you aren't Matt's girl-griend—and I say *girl*-friend with the full meaning of the word. You can't bear for a man to touch you, can you? Or is it only me you have this aversion to?'

She held herself stiffly, her blonde hair falling untidily about her shoulders. 'I would like to say it's only you, Mr Gregory, but I'm afraid it isn't. I have yet to find the man who can raise me to the heights of passion or put me in the depths of despair—if such feelings exist, which I doubt.'

André Gregory's attention seemed to be fixed on

the ornaments on the dressing-table, as he picked up first one object and then another. 'I think you could be right,' he agreed, not bothering to look at her. 'Oh, the heights of passion exist all right, but the depths of despair have so far eluded me. Possibly because so far, like you, I have no wish to give one single person the power to make my life either happy or sad for me.'

'But then even in that we differ. You see, you don't have one person in your life, but several, whereas I don't have any.'

'Don't you believe in the old saying "safety in numbers"?'

She shook her head. 'Not for me. Now I really do have to go and dress.'

'As I recall, you haven't apologised yet,' he reminded her softly.

'No, and I'm not going to.'

'Oh, but you are.' Steely fingers gripped her arm once again. 'And right now. Go on, say you're sorry like a good girl.'

Caroline's eyes glittered resentfully. How dared he! Just who did he think he was! The impulse to tell him who *she* was was strong, but she resisted. He hadn't been insulting enough yet to be intimidated by the knowledge that she was Matt Rayner's daughter, and not his—not his girl-friend. Her temper kindled anew at this slight on her father's conduct. Just because this man didn't care who he made love to it didn't mean her father was the same. 'I have nothing to apologise for, you were obstructing my exit and I asked you to move.'

His teeth gleamed whitely as he grinned at her. 'You didn't *ask* me to do anything, young lady, you gave me an order. And I don't like orders, especially from women. I'm still waiting,' he said patiently.

'Well, you can go on waiting,' she fumed at him.

'Because I'm never going to apologise to you—I repeat, *never*!'

André Gregory continued to look down at her, his expression just as unyielding as her own. 'There was no need to repeat it, Caroline, I heard you the first time. But you will apologise,' he looked about them pointedly, finally resting his steely gaze back on her flushed face. 'You're hardly in a position to argue. Must I remind you of your surroundings, and your dress—or in this case, *un*dress? I could so easily take advantage of this situation—but I'm sure you wouldn't like me to do that.'

'You wouldn't dare!' she challenged.

'Wouldn't I? Well, perhaps you're right. Matt's a friend of mine, and you're——'

'His preserve,' Caroline cut in tautly. 'But I'm not, Mr Gregory. Oh, all right,' she sighed. 'If it inflates your male ego to force a defenceless girl to apologise—I apologise. Satisfied?'

He released her arm. 'For a moment there I thought you were going to admit your relationship with Matt, but perhaps you're not the sort of girl to go around boasting of your conquests.'

'Conquests!' she scoffed, rubbing her bruised wrist where he had held her so tightly. 'You call being the mistress of a middle-aged tycoon a conquest? I wouldn't! I'd call it——'

'I think I can guess what you would call it, Little Miss Puritan. Where's the harm in bringing a little happiness into someone's life? Or do you also object to that? God, what a little prude you are! And what a curious combination, prudishness and promiscuity.'

'Promiscuity? But I'm not——'

'Not you, Caroline, Cynthia or whatever her name is. Do you lecture her too?'

Caroline turned away. 'She happens to be a friend of mine, and I speak with full authority when I say she is not promiscuous. Far from it, in fact.'

'So the stories I've heard are unfounded, are they?'

She resented his taunting tone, shaking her long hair back haughtily. 'As I have no idea what these stories are I can't really say, but I would advise you not to listen to idle gossip, Mr Gregory. I would have thought you of all people would have known that what people don't know they *think* they know, or simply make it up.'

'Me of all people? Oh, I see—you mean someone of my tendencies, my friends' wives and so forth? Mmm, well, in some cases perhaps what you say is true, but I happen to have received my information on good authority.

'And what authority is that?' she asked sharply.

'Now that would be telling,' he replied, infuriatingly calm, appraising her appearance once again. 'And if you don't go and dress in a moment I may take your reluctance to leave my bedroom as an invitation—and I may just accept.'

'Don't excite yourself, Mr Gregory, I wouldn't invite you anywhere, let alone into my bed!' and she made her escape before he decided to make her apologise for that remark too, locking herself safely in the bathroom. She leaned heavily on the door, listening for his movements. To her chagrin he was merrily whistling to himself as he went down the stairs. Did nothing ruffle that smooth surface charm he chose to emit? Well, she would do her hardest to find out. Mr André Gregory needed taking down a peg or two, and she was just the person to do it.

She could smell bacon cooking as she walked gracefully down the stairs—her bacon, no doubt. Really, that man had a nerve! 'Hi,' she smiled happily at him as she sat down at the kitchen table, showing none of the seething emotions that existed underneath. 'Are you cooking enough for me?'

If he was surprised by her change of attitude he didn't show it, but gave her a cursory glance before carrying on with his frying. 'If you want some,' he said noncommittally.

'Thanks.' Caroline leant her chin on her hands, her blue eyes full of mischief if he bothered to look at her, which he didn't. 'Country air always makes me ravenous, doesn't it you?'

'I suppose so,' he agreed quietly. 'I'm not usually in the country long enough to find out one way or the other.' He turned to face her. 'So—when are you leaving?'

Caroline's pleasant manner almost deserted her at his audacity, but she managed to remain cool. 'Leaving?' she repeated. 'Oh, I'm not leaving,' she told him sweetly. 'As you so rightly said last night, there are two bedrooms and I won't bother you if you don't bother me.'

He studied her for a moment, the expression in his green eyes unreadable. 'Are you quite serious?'

'Quite,' she mocked. 'Why not? It could work out very well if we let it.'

'Caroline, I came here for peace and quiet. I'm hardly likely to get that with you walking about half undressed most of the time and in very revealing tight jumpers and denims at other times. Hardly conducive to a peaceful existence, hmm?'

'Are you saying you find me attractive, Mr Gregory?'

'No, I didn't say that, not *you* especially. It would be impossible for any man not to be slightly disturbed by your appearance.' He placed a laden breakfast plate before her. 'So I repeat—when are you leaving?'

She tucked enthusiastically into the crisp bacon and perfectly fried egg. 'And I repeat—I'm not. Look, Mr Gregory—André,' she saw his start of surprise and the narrowing of those sea-green eyes, and smiled slightly to herself. 'I'll be in the studio most of the time, so you can do—whatever it is you want to do, down here. Surely that's a perfectly feasible idea?'

'Oh, it's feasible all right, it's just that I'm not agreeable to it. I came here to get away from—charming females like yourself, not to set up home with one. Anyway, why the sudden change of heart? A few moments ago you couldn't wait to get rid of me.'

'I've been thinking while I was upstairs, and I decided that there was no need for this unpleasantness. This cottage is big enough for two people—just, and we needn't interfere with each other in any way.'

'And what do you think Matt will say to that?' he queried.

'I've already told him. Ah, that surprises you, doesn't it? Yes, I told—Matt, that I was staying on here, just as you probably told him you were. He wasn't very happy about the arrangement, but he'll come round.'

His mouth twisted. 'Oh, I'm sure he will. You have your own little ways of getting to him, I suppose. Oh, eat your breakfast, and we'll talk about it later,' he added impatiently.

Caroline did as she was told, enjoying the meal he had cooked for her. Let him try and puzzle out her change of attitude for himself. She had deliberately chosen to wear a blue jumper that exactly matched the colour of her eyes and showed off her long blonde hair to advantage, intending to disconcert him. And she had succeeded! Well, watch out, André Gregory, because it had only just started. Before she had finished she would get him so intrigued by her behaviour that he would wonder what had hit him. And *then* would come the let-down. Oh yes, Mr Conceited Gregory, your time has come, she vowed silently.

She settled down in the studio to do some preliminary drawings. It was a long time since she had been to the cottage and she always found she could relax and paint better here than anywhere else. But this morning she seemed to be having some trouble settling down to any serious work, and put that down to the fact that she could hear André Gregory moving about downstairs. She wondered what he could possibly be doing. Finally, when she thought she could stand it no longer, he called up the stairs to her.

'Caroline! Caroline, Matt's on the telephone for you.'

She put down her equipment and rushed to the studio door. 'Did you say Matt?' she asked breathlessly.

He stood at the bottom of the stairs looking up at her. 'I did, and I think it's quite urgent.'

'Oh, okay. Can you put the call through up here? Just press the switch on the side of the telephone,' she explained.

'Do you have any objection to speaking to him in front of me?' his eyes taunted.

'Certainly I do. My conversation with Mr Rayner is private.'

'I see. And you still maintain there's nothing between the two of you.' His smile was frankly mocking as he moved out of her line of vision.

Caroline was tempted to flounce down the stairs and give him a piece of her mind, but was prevented from doing so by the buzzing of the telephone behind her. Bother the man! She snatched up the receiver, her mouth set in a mutinous line. It was going to be much more difficult to be pleasant to André Gregory than she had imagined. 'Yes?' she said sharply.

'Caroline?' her father's gruff voice enquired. 'Has something upset you?'

She laughed softly at his understatement. 'Only your arrogant friend, nothing I can't handle.'

Now it was his turn to laugh. 'If you believe that, Caroline, then you certainly don't know André very well. Some of the most self-assured women in the world have tried to manage him, and failed. I can't see that you'll succeed where so many others have failed.'

'I'm not intending to marry the man, Daddy, just teach him a lesson he's badly in need of.'

'Caroline, you just don't understand, or you don't *want* to understand. André is not the man to try tricks like this on. And why did I have to just ask for Caroline and not for my daughter?'

'Because for the moment that is the one thing I'm not, although according to your friend I'm plenty of other things.'

'Like what?'

She bit her lip thoughtfully. 'I know—your mistress, for one thing.'

'My *what*!'

She laughed at his astonishment. 'Your mistress,' she repeated. 'Besides being a member of the permissive society.'

'Damn cheek of the man!' came the mumbled reply.

'Oh, come off it, Daddy, wouldn't you think the same in the circumstances?'

'No, I wouldn't.'

'Daddy!'

'Well ... perhaps. But he has a nerve suggesting something like that. What does he think I am, a cradle-snatcher?'

'There isn't that much difference between your age and Greg Fortnum's, and you thought we would be well suited,' she pointed out reasonably. 'Anyway, he said I shouldn't be ashamed of bringing a little happiness into someone's life, *your* life.'

'Big of him!'

'That's what I thought. So I'm going to pay him back for it. By the time I've finished with him he may not have quite such an inflated ego,' she said with relish.

'Caroline, I wouldn't advise——'

'Don't worry, Daddy. I'll leave before things get too hot, but I really do think your pushy friend needs his ego knocked down a bit.'

'Well, all right, if that's what you want to do, but it's against my advice. And if it gets out to the press that you're living out in the wilds with André Gregory your reputation will be in shreds.'

'It won't get out, there's no reason why it should.'

'I suppose not,' he mumbled. 'But I want you to keep in touch with me.'

'Of course I will, but not too often. How can I play the seductress if he thinks I'm involved with you?'

'Play the seductress?' he queried sharply. 'Now, Caroline, that isn't a good idea.'

'Why not? I can assure you that there's absolutely no risk of my actually falling for him. He's just an arrogant, bossy prig. And I'm going to bring him to his knees!'

She heard her father laugh. 'I wish you luck,' he chuckled before ringing off.

Caroline stared at the telephone for a moment before gently replacing it back on its stand. Her father hadn't taken her plans too badly under the circumstances, and she was looking forward to teaching André Gregory a lesson. But she had to go carefully or he would become suspicious. But there was no time like the present to start her plan.

The man so much in her thoughts of late was sitting back comfortably in an armchair before the warm fire, his bare feet roasting in front of the flames. A cigar burnt slowly between his slender fingers and his attention seemed to be wholly on the book he was reading.

She sat impishly before him on the carpet, instantly feeling the heat of the fire. 'Is it good?' she asked huskily.

The book slowly lowered and a pair of deceptively

sleepy green eyes looked at her over its top. 'Very good,' he replied shortly.

'I've read quite a lot of Alistair Maclean books myself. But I haven't read that one,' she tried to draw him into conversation.

'You can have it when I've finished it. Perhaps it will keep you out of trouble for a while.' He returned his attention to the book.

Caroline put out a hand and lowered it again. 'Couldn't you talk to me?'

He raised dark eyebrows. 'Now what could we possibly have to say to one another? As far as I know we have nothing in common.'

She grinned at him. 'That isn't quite true, we have Alistair Maclean. Now that's a start, wouldn't you say?'

A smile tugged at the corners of his mouth. 'Perhaps,' he conceded. 'But it isn't very encouraging, is it?'

She stood up with enthusiasm. 'Come shopping with me,' she invited gaily.

'What?'

'Come shopping with me.' She took his book out of his hands and tried to pull him to his feet. 'I'll buy you steak and cook it for you with my own fair hands,' she said enticingly when he resisted her efforts.

'Is that supposed to encourage me?' he asked dryly.

'Mm,' she grinned. 'I cook steak divinely.'

'I only have your word for that.' He stood languidly to his feet, tucking his shirt back into the low waistband of his faded denims.

'But I can, truthfully.'

'Right, I'll believe you. Get your coat and we'll go out.'

'Oh, lovely,' she smiled.

André's eyes narrowed thoughtfully. 'Why this sudden partiality for my company? I'm sure Matt was full of how dark my intentions are if I'm encouraged.'

'And even if you're not encouraged too,' she laughed. 'And as you're the only other person here I can hardly have a partiality for anyone else's company.'

'True.' He put out his cigar. 'What did Matt say about your staying on here with me?'

'He wished me luck.'

'What did he mean by that?'

'I haven't the faintest idea,' she lied. 'But I suppose he meant that he hopes I behave myself—not that I don't normally,' she added hastily.

'I'm sure,' he said dryly. 'Innocent girls, like you profess to be, often stay in deserted cottages with complete strangers. I realise it's done all the time.'

Caroline held on to her temper with difficulty, pouting prettily at his brooding expression. 'You aren't a *complete* stranger.'

'Oh no, I forgot, you're the mistress of one of my best friends. That makes you an acquaintance of mine too, I suppose?'

'You're not being very nice to me,' she said sulkily.

'Am I not?'

'You know you're not.'

'Maybe.' André picked up his jacket from the chair. 'But I don't trust people who don't fit into my first impressions of them.'

'And I don't?'

André shook his head, his eyes flickering appreciatively over her slim body. 'Afraid not. One minute you're spitting like a wildcat, and the next you're purring like a kitten.'

Caroline's eyes sparkled mischievously. 'I thought men liked variety in their women.'

He grinned, tapping her sharply on the bottom to usher her out of the room. 'We do,' he agreed. 'But not all in the same woman.'

She held back her angry retort at his familiarity, and

ran quickly up the stairs to collect her coat while he put on his shoes.

The man below watched her with narrowed eyes, conscious of the deliberate swaying of perfectly curved hips.

CHAPTER THREE

THEY came out of the foodstore, their arms laden with groceries. Caroline giggled. 'I think we have enough food here to feed an army for a week!'

'Mm,' André agreed, looking at her over a bag full of shopping. 'You shouldn't have brought me out with an empty stomach.'

'I like that!' she laughed. 'You had your breakfast not two hours ago.' Surprisingly she had enjoyed her shopping expedition with this almost total stranger. It had been fun, and she couldn't believe the amount of food they had collected when they eventually got to the checkout. André Gregory had insisted on paying for it all, insisting that as she was going to do the cooking it was only fair that he paid for the food. 'Oh, look,' she exclaimed, pointing to a stall that sold ice-cream. 'Can I have one?' she looked at him beguilingly.

His look was one of amused tolerance. 'Okay, but let's get rid of these things first and then have a decent one in that café.'

Caroline watched him beneath lowered lashes as he drank his preferred coffee. 'My treat,' she had urged, but still he declined the ice-cream. She hadn't let his refusal deter her, and ordered a huge banana split for herself. She paused in her enjoyment. 'It's typical of me,' she smiled, her blue eyes warm, her hostility towards this man momentarily forgotten. 'It's freezing cold outside,' she explained, 'and here I am eating ice-cream.'

'Typical woman,' was his only comment.

'And that, Mr Gregory, is a typical male chauvinistic comment.'

'Why the formality? We are living together, after all,' he chuckled wryly as Caroline looked hurriedly around the crowded café to see if anyone had overheard his comment. 'Don't worry, no one heard. But if our accommodation arrangement leaked out to anyone that's the obvious conclusion they would come to.'

'Well, that just shows how wrong they would be,' she retorted tartly.

'Oh, I realise that, but would Matt like that kind of publicity?'

'I won't profess to know what you mean.'

André shrugged his shoulders, the denim jacket he wore moulded to his powerful frame. 'Well, if I deny any relationship between the two of us they'll obviously wonder where you fit into the arrangement. Oh, I know you say you're a friend of Matt's daughter, but can you honestly see anyone else believing we would stay here together in the circumstances?'

'No, but then I don't particularly care for other people's opinions. Or do you have someone of importance in your life at the moment who might take exception to us staying together?' She waited with bated breath, then shook herself mentally for acting so stupidly.

For a moment he was silent. 'Yes, there could be someone of importance, but somehow I don't think she'll mind.'

'She won't?'

André shook his head. 'I'm sure of it.'

'Isn't she the possessive type, or doesn't she share your feelings?' although she didn't think it could be the latter, even she had to admit he was devastatingly attractive, and when he looked at her a certain way her pulse began to beat erratically. And she didn't even like him! What effect he would have on someone who actually wanted him she wouldn't like to think.

'You're singularly inquisitive today, Caroline.'

'Sorry,' she coloured. 'I didn't mean to pry.'

'Yes, you did,' he said softly. 'And the answer is the latter. I would think she hardly knows of my existence.' He watched the play of emotions across her face and could imagine the numerous questions she was longing to ask. He laughed at her forbearance. 'Your thoughts are very clear, Caroline, but I'm not going to satisfy that female curiosity of yours. It will give you something to think about.'

'I have plenty to occupy me,' she snapped at him, grinning reluctantly at his teasing expression. 'But I am curious,' she admitted. 'I would have thought that anyone you——' She broke off as she realised she was about to be rude to him again.

André stood up in preparation of leaving. 'Once I set out to get someone they wouldn't escape my clutches, right?'

Caroline had the grace to blush. 'Well, I——'

'It's not important.' He laid a handful of silver on the table for the coffee and ice-cream, silencing her as she would have protested. 'You can pay the next time we come.'

'But we may not come back again, and I did say it was my treat.'

'We'll be back,' he promised. 'I can't see either of us staying at the cottage for the next few weeks without a break.'

'From each other, you mean?'

'Not necessarily. I've found you very entertaining so far, and I see no reason for that to change. I wait in anticipation for your next move,' he mocked.

He propelled her towards the car, opening the door for her to get in before getting in beside her. Close to him like this Caroline found his proximity overpowering and she moved slightly away from him. He drove the car with all the confidence that she had known he would, and she couldn't help but admire his quick decisive movements on the steering wheel.

'What next move?' she asked innocently.

'The next outrageous thing you're going to do. You change like the wind, so I should think you're going to lose your temper over something next.'

'I don't have a temper,' she said firmly.

'No, because you keep losing it,' he taunted.

'Are you trying to antagonise me, André?'

He grinned at her deliberate use of his first name. 'I don't need to try, I seem to do it quite naturally.' The tires of the car swished to a halt in front of the cottage. 'Quite an accomplishment really.' He opened the door for her as they took the shopping into the kitchen, studying her as she began to deftly put it away. 'You know your way around here pretty well, don't you?'

Caroline ran her hands nervously down her tight denims, looking at his face for any sign of a double meaning to his words. 'Pretty well,' she agreed finally. 'I stay here often.'

'With Matt?'

'And his daughter.'

'But there are only two bedrooms,' he pointed out. 'Which bedroom do you share, Matt's or his daughter's?'

'You're despicable!' Her eyes sparkled angrily and she banged a tin down with force on the table. 'Mr Rayner is a fine, decent man.'

'Okay, okay,' he put up a protesting hand. 'I'm tired of baiting you. But I'll draw my own conclusions about that set-up,' he went to the kitchen door, 'and for what it's worth, I wouldn't blame him.'

'Thanks for nothing!' She heard his mocking laughter as he left the room. She banged about the kitchen preparing their lunch.

'What happened to the steak?' André looked up from his book to the sandwiches she placed beside him.

'That's for dinner,' Caroline said shortly, biting angrily into her own sandwich.

'By candlelight, no doubt.'

'If you want,' she answered ungraciously. 'Is there anything wrong with your sandwiches?'

'No, they're fine.' He stood up. 'Do you want a beer?'

'No, thanks.'

He came back with two cans of beer and settled himself down again beside the fire. Caroline glared at him resentfully, her good humour momentarily forgotten. André looked up finally, as if her unflinching stare had finally penetrated his cold shell.

'Is there anything wrong?' he asked mildly.

She shook her head, red lights from the flames in the fire shining in her blonde hair. 'Not particularly, but you aren't very good company.'

'I didn't come here with the intention of entertaining an adolescent twenty-four hours a day.'

Caroline ignored his reference to her being an adolescent. 'Hardly twenty-four hours a day,' she said dryly. 'Don't you want to talk to me?'

'Not particularly,' he sighed heavily. 'All right. So what do your parents think of you living all over the place like this?'

'I don't! And I only have a father.'

'Then it's a pity he doesn't take better care of you,' he told her shortly.

'He takes perfectly good care of me. But I'm old enough to take care of myself anyway.'

'And how old is that?'

'You shouldn't ask a woman her age.'

'But you say you aren't a woman in the fullest sense—yet. So what is the great age?'

'Twenty.'

'Twenty!' he scoffed.

'There's nothing wrong with being twenty—you

were once,' she answered huffily.

'Mm,' he gave a slight smile. 'And now I'm thirty-seven. That must seem very old to a baby like you.'

She shook her head. 'No, I like older men,' she told him truthfully.

André laughed. 'If I didn't know you better, Caro, my dear, I would say you were flirting with me, out-rageously.'

Caroline kept her eyes lowered, her fingers plucking nervously at the fluffy carpet. She had liked the way he shortened her name, no one had ever done that before, and it sounded curiously intimate coming from this man. 'Perhaps I am,' she said huskily.

'I doubt it,' André said harshly. 'Don't start something you can't finish, Caro. I'm not a little boy that you can tease and then tell to go to hell.'

'Is that what you think I am? A little tease?' Somehow the words hurt.

'Well, aren't you? One minute you can't stand the sight of me and the next you can't get enough of my company. Oh, don't worry, I don't take you seri-ously, but some other poor devil might.'

'Oh!' She stood angrily to her feet. 'You're hor-rible!' She slammed out of the room, hurriedly picking up her coat and letting herself out of the cottage. In-sufferable man! Her first impression of him had been the correct one.

The air was fresh and invigorating and she walked for miles. It was her first opportunity to rid herself of the cobwebs of London and she enjoyed every moment of the freedom the barrenness of the country-side gave her. The trees were bare of leaves and there was hardly any colour anywhere, but strangely enough Caroline loved it all. She sat down on the top of a tiny hill and surveyed the beauty of her surroundings. There was nothing like the peace and tranquillity she could find here anywhere else in the world.

Among the other country noises there was a noise that shouldn't have been there, a tiny cry, like an animal in pain. She stood up, looking anxiously around for the poor animal, but could see nothing. Then a slight movement to the left caught her eye and bending down on her haunches she saw the cause of the cry. Looking up at her with frightened blue eyes was a tiny black kitten; which was so young that it couldn't even miaow properly yet, only squeak. She guessed it must be about four or five weeks old, although it was very tiny for its age, seeming all ears and eyes.

'Hello, little girl,' she crooned softly, putting out a hand slowly so as not to frighten the poor little creature. The kitten flinched as if it was about to be struck and Caroline spoke soothingly to it until it calmed down again. Before it could run away her hand shot out and clasped the tiny thing about its stomach, feeling its tiny ribs sticking out. 'Oh, you little darling,' she crooned. 'You're starving to death out here!' She looked about her, but there was no sign of habitation anywhere in sight. 'How long have you been lost, my little baby? Mm?'

The kitten, realising that at last it had found someone who was kind, snuggled down into the warmth of her arms, its little face trusting. Caroline held it as gently as she could, realising how delicate it was in its hunger. Its fur wasn't fluffy and soft as it should have been, but rough and matted, and Caroline could only assume it had been lost for several days. 'How would you like to come home with me, Susi?'

For answer the kitten sighed and closed its eyes, rocked to sleep by the steady walk back to the cottage. Caroline had it wrapped up in her arms to shield off the biting wind, and it only stirred slightly as they entered the warmth of the cottage before settling down more comfortably within the protection of her arms.

The lounge door swung open with a thud and

André Gregory stood silhouetted in the warm glow that could be seen from the fire. 'Where the hell do you——?' He broke off, becoming aware of the tiny bundle of fur in her arms. 'What's that?'

Caroline looked up at him. 'It's a kitten,' she answered softly, careful not to wake the sleeping creature. 'And I think it's nearly dead,' she choked over the last word.

André came forward softly, peeping at the tiny object in her arms. 'Where did you find it?'

'Out in the hills.' She looked at him appealingly, her eyes swimming with unshed tears. 'Oh, André, she won't die, will she?'

'I don't know.' He took the kitten from her gently, looking closely at its thin body. 'Get some warm milk and we'll see what we can do.' She still stared at the kitten. 'Caro, get the milk, there's a good girl.'

She roused herself enough to run into the kitchen to warm some milk. André had placed the kitten before the warm fire by the time she entered the lounge with the milk, stroking the now warm body as it slept. He took the saucer from her shaking hands, placing it encouragingly before the little black nose. The kitten didn't move.

'I'll have to wake it,' he said finally. 'It isn't going to wake itself, and I think it needs food more than sleep at the moment.' He gently woke up the kitten, facing it towards the milk. The little black nose gave a twitch, but the kitten made no move to drink the milk.

'Oh, André,' cried Caroline, 'it won't eat!'

'Don't panic, Caroline,' He stroked the kitten absently, receiving a few half-hearted licks for his efforts. 'That's it!' he said suddenly. 'I saw a film once with the same circumstances, only then it was a lion.' He dipped his fingers into the milk and put it near the kitten's mouth. It gave one tentative lick, then another, until André's finger was completely bare of milk. He put the saucer closer to the small body and watched with satisfaction as the little pink tongue licked at the milk hungrily. 'There,' he smiled, standing up to stretch his long legs.

'Oh, André,' she launched herself into his arms, hugging him tightly around his waist. 'Thank you, thank you!'

'Hey!' he laughed softly, holding her gently away from him. 'I'm horrible, remember?'

Caroline looked slightly abashed. 'That was before.'

'Now I'm not so bad, huh?' There was a curious stillness about him and she looked up at him questioningly. Her eyes lowered again under the force of those startling green ones, conscious that for an unguarded moment she had seen desire flame in those eyes, desire that was quickly hidden, so quickly she wondered if she had seen it at all. His hands dropped away from her. 'So why did you disappear like that?'

'Don't tell me you were worried?'

'A little,' he admitted ruefully. 'So how about that dinner now?'

'I can't. I have to go back into the village and get some fish and chicken for the kitten.'

'I'll go, you cook.'

'Are you by any chance hungry?' she teased.

'Ravenous,' he laughed, tickling the kitten playfully under its fluffy chin. 'I won't be long,' he promised.

'Right.' Caroline set about preparing dinner with a feeling of excess happiness. She couldn't explain this feeling, except that the kitten was going to be all right, and André was being nice to her again. She stopped what she was doing. Why should André being kind to her make her feel happy? She didn't know why, but then perhaps she didn't want to know.

She prepared the mushroom sauce for the steak, placed the salad in the centre of the table, and cooked up new potatoes to accompany the meal. Cheese and biscuits would have to do for a dessert; after all, she hadn't professed to be a fantastic cook.

She heard André return just as she was changing and quickly zipped up the velvet evening pants she had chosen to wear before hurrying down the stairs. She wore a matching velvet waistcoat in the same shade of royal blue, and knew that the colour darkened her eyes and lightened her already blonde hair. She wore no blouse under the waistcoat, knowing that it suited her more to have bare arms and throat, her skin appearing palely fragile against the darkness of the blue.

André was in the kitchen feeding the kitten its chicken when she came in, and Caroline had an opportunity to study him without being observed. There was no doubt that he was an extremely handsome specimen, there was something about him that was completely *male*, with an air of self-assurance many women must have appreciated before her. He couldn't possibly have lived thirty-seven years without capitalising on that magnetism, in fact she was sure he had—hadn't he admitted as much to her at their first meeting?

He looked up, catching her unawares, and Caroline blushed guiltily. His eyes passed slowly down the long length of her body, pausing for long breathless seconds on the lowness of her neckline where the firm swell of her totally matured breasts could be clearly seen. Caroline had given up wearing bras during the heat of the summer just passed, and had not thought it necessary to recommence wearing such a cumbersome article of clothing. She felt sure that her lack of clothing wasn't missed by those piercing green eyes, and for the first time she could ever remember she felt like covering up her body, away from those all-seeing eyes.

André straightened up from the cooker, his eyes now shielded by long lashes. 'To what do I owe the pleasure of your charming attire, and pleasure it undoubtedly is?'

Caroline blushed again and then mentally remonstrated with herself. What had happened to all that poise and self-confidence she had been taught at finishing school? 'I don't know what you mean,' she said flippantly. 'Isn't it the usual practice to change for dinner?'

'Mmm,' his eyes glowed with a warmth she found unnerving. 'But have you any idea of the change you've made?'

'Don't be silly,' she said nervously. 'I'm still wearing trousers and a top.'

'If you say so.' He took a step towards her. 'Look after the kitten's food while I go and change too, will you? I can't have you shaming me.'

'I'm sure I could never do that,' Caroline returned sweetly, picking the kitten up from the floor where it had tired itself out exploring, and was now unsuccessfully trying to make itself comfortable on the vinyl floor. She looked at him over the safety of two little black ears. 'Dinner in fifteen minutes.'

André took the stairs two at a time. 'I'll be down in ten,' he promised mockingly.

She placed the steaks under the grill to cook and the mushroom sauce on to simmer while she made a makeshift basket for Susi. It didn't take her long to cut a hole out of the side of the box they had brought their shopping home in, and with one of Caroline's old tee-shirts left over from the summer tucked into the bottom, Susi was soon fast asleep before the roasting fire. Caroline returned to the kitchen, covering the steak with the delicious sauce. She had just served the steaks on to the plates when André returned downstairs.

If he had been surprised by her appearance she was even more so by his. Dressed completely in black, from the clinging silk shirt to the snug-fitting trousers. He had the look of a devil, a devil whose eyes glowed emerald green in his darkly tanned face.

'Don't you ever wear shoes?' she asked tremulously, clutching on to the first sane thought that came into her head. But perhaps it wasn't so sane. The fact that he chose to walk about like that gave their relationship an intimacy it just didn't possess.

'Not if I can help it,' he grinned. 'Does it offend you?'

'Would it matter if it did?'

'Maybe,' he replied enigmatically. 'Does it?'

Caroline flicked back her hair nervously. 'No,' she said firmly. 'Are you ready for your dinner now?'

'Yes, please, and may I say it smells delicious.'

'You may,' she smiled almost shyly. 'Go through and I'll bring these in a moment.' When she had recovered her equilibrium, she thought dryly. Her father had been right to warn her of this man's devastating charm; if she wasn't careful she might even find herself falling for him. But that wouldn't do at all! This man already had enough of an inflated ego without any encouragement from her.

It was disconcerting to find that André had taken her at her word and put lighted candles on the table, turning off the main electric light and casting dark shadows over the room. With any other man Caroline might have found the setting romantic, with this man it was downright dangerous. But what could she say without giving him the satisfaction of knowing he had some effect on her?

The green eyes mocked her as she placed his laden plate before him without making contact with his firm warm body. She was increasingly conscious of the clean male smell of him, concentrating her whole attention on her own meal.

André leant forward and poured her out a glass of wine. For preparing this appetising meal,' he explained at her enquiring look.

'But you didn't know it would be.'

'Sure I did. You wouldn't tell me you were good at something if you weren't confident that you were.'

'How do you know that?'

'You aren't the type.' He tasted the juicy steak. 'Mmm, lovely. Where did you learn to make the sauce? It's superb.'

'We were taught that sort of thing at school,' she informed him, secretly pleased by his praise, although remaining outwardly cool.

'Finishing school, no doubt?'

Caroline sipped at her wine appreciatively, knowing in her limited experience that it had been chosen to accompany steak. She raised enquiring eyebrows. 'Why do you say that?'

'Because you have the air of a "finished" young lady. Anyway, isn't that where you met Matt's daughter, and consequently Matt himself?'

Caroline shook her head. 'I've known—Cynthia all my life. We were at school together.'

André smiled mockingly. 'I see. But I doubt if that young lady can cook like this. I'm sure she had better things to do with her time than learn how to cook.'

Caroline's mouth tightened angrily. 'I believe you said you'd never met her?' she said sweetly.

'I was going to once.'

'Then why didn't you?' She still couldn't understand why she had never heard her father mention this man before, especially as they seemed to know each other so well.

'I managed to get out of it. Matt's intention of finding a husband for his daughter is very obvious, and from that observation I can only suppose the poor girl isn't as attractive as she could be,' he laughed softly. 'She probably has buck-teeth and spots.'

'Don't be absurd!'

'Okay then, what does she look like?'

'Well, she——' Caroline hesitated. 'She looks rather like me.'

'Impossible. There couldn't be two like you.'

'What do you mean?'

'Good question.' He became thoughtful, studying her intensely. 'You have an unusual beauty, a beauty that couldn't possibly be copied.'

She blushed self-consciously. 'Blonde hair and blue eyes are hardly original,' she scoffed to cover her embarrassment, becoming more and more aware of her precarious position alone in this lonely cottage with a man she hardly knew. She smiled at him mockingly. 'If I didn't know you better, Mr Gregory, I would say you were flirting with me,' she tauntingly repeated his words of this afternoon. '*Outrageously,*' she added teasingly.

Deep green eyes ravaged the beauty of her face and body. 'Perhaps I am,' he agreed huskily.

It wasn't the answer she had expected, and standing up to shield her nervousness she bent down to study the exhausted but contented kitten still nestled inside the box. She couldn't bear to sit at the table and have André Gregory taunting her with his devastating masculinity. There was something unbearably intimate about this dinner that had started out so innocently, at least, on her part. But surely no situation like this could ever be innocent, and she at last became aware of the danger of her position.

Finally she looked up. 'Do you think Susi will be all right now?'

André picked up their two wine glasses and came to sit beside her near the fire. He handed her her still half-full glass. 'Susi?'

'The kitten,' she explained.

'Oh, I see. Changing the subject.'

'You were becoming too personal,' she said tartly.

André laughed softly, his look warm and caressing in the candlelight. 'That isn't your real reason. I've said much more personal things to you and you haven't reacted to them at all. Why should the fact that I find you attractive upset you?'

'That wasn't what upset me, although I do find it rather hard to believe. It was merely the fact that you were trying to flatter me into falling for your charm.'

'Flattering you? I most certainly was not. You *are* unusual in your beauty, the fact that you don't think yourself attractive is unusual in itself. Your hair is like sunlight and silver moonlight entwined together, and you have the creamiest complexion I've seen on any woman. And as for your eyes! They're huge blue lakes that a man could lose his soul in.'

Caroline put her hands over her ears. 'No! I won't— I can't listen to you.'

'Why not?' he asked softly.

'Because you—you don't really mean it.'

André slowly put down his glass, his eyes holding her spellbound as he came down on the fluffy goatskin rug beside her. He put out one of his strong hands and gently touched her warm cheek. 'But I do, Caro,' he whispered softly. 'I mean every word of it.'

Suddenly his dark head bent and his lips claimed hers in a manner that could only be described as sensuous. His lips rubbed tantalisingly against her own until almost against her will her lips opened to receive the warmth of his kiss. For long seconds she resisted him, until the urgency of his lips and hands broke down her defences and she found herself returning his caresses with an abandon that surprised her.

His mouth left her lips to travel seductively down

her neck to her shoulder and on down to the deep
shadow cast between her breasts. 'Caro,' he groaned,
his hands travelling under the tightness of her velvet
waistcoat to caress the firm pointed flesh beneath. 'Stop
me. For God's sake, stop me!'

Caroline was lost in the vortex of their passion and
she realised that this was where all their verbal fencing
had inevitably been leading to. 'I don't want to,' she
told him huskily, her hands unbuttoning the silk shirt
that clung to him like a second skin, her fingers exploring the dampness of his skin.

With a deep groan André reclaimed her lips and
she felt his fingers move to the four pearl buttons that
were the only fastening to her waistcoat. She knew
herself lost, no sign of resistance coming from her.
'Caro, Caro,' he muttered her name endlessly even
while his lips sought the firmness of her youthful body,
taking the tip of one full breast between parted lips.
Her groans of pleasure only incited him to more
frenzied caresses and she gave herself up to the feelings
of intense pleasure that were racking her body.

It was the shrill insistent sound of the telephone
ringing that finally invaded their clamouring senses,
and with a groan André raised himself above her still
lethargic body and snatched the offending instrument
from its cradle. 'Yes!' he snapped into the receiver,
his eyes still stormy and glazed from aroused passion.
'Hang on a moment,' he said, slamming the telephone
down on the table. 'It's for you,' he said coldly. 'Your
boy-friend.'

Caroline was doing her best to refasten the small
pearl buttons with hands that shook uncontrollably.
'B—boy-friend?' she asked dazedly.

'Matt,' André replied uncompromisingly, pushing
her hands away and fastening the buttons himself.
'Can't have you talking to one man when you look
as if you've just left the arms of another one, even if

you have,' he added cruelly.

'Do you—do you have to mock just now?' she asked shakily.

'What else would you suggest I do?' he demanded harshly. 'Tell Matt to go to the devil as I'd like to do? What happens then? We resume where we left off? I think not!'

She looked at him with hurt blue eyes, picking up the telephone with shaking hands. 'Yes?' she said softly, her senses still aflame with what had almost happened. If her father hadn't—— But he had! And only just in time.

'Caroline?' Her father sounded worried. 'Did I interrupt anything just now?'

She looked over to where André now stood completely composed, a fresh glass of wine in his hand, his expression shuttered. 'No,' she said shakily, 'You didn't interrupt anything.' She saw André's head snap back angrily. 'Nothing of importance,' she added hurtfully.

'Oh, only André sounded rather put out.'

Caroline avoided looking at the other occupant of the room. 'André just lost something, but it wasn't really that important. I'm sure he'll soon find another one,' she said chokingly.

'What are you talking about?' He sounded impatient.

'It isn't important,' she replied evasively. 'Did you want something?'

'Only to know if my daughter still has her virginal innocence,' he said dryly. 'I trust you have?' he asked worriedly.

She managed a light laugh. 'Which of us don't you trust?'

'Look, Caroline, I'm only concerned about you. Men of André's calibre don't usually enter your safe little world.'

She was very conscious of André listening to her conversation, and although there was a lot she would have liked to say to reassure her father a lot of it simply wouldn't be true. André *was* different from any other man she had ever met, something she had almost discovered to her cost this evening. And it wasn't even his fault! He had almost begged her to stop him. She sighed deeply. 'No, you're right. And I promise that in future I'll be more careful.'

'In future?' her father queried sharply. 'Does that mean something has already happened?'

'No,' she denied quickly, perhaps too quickly. 'Nothing that I can't handle.' She looked up to meet green taunting eyes and looked away again quickly. 'It's getting late now, I think I should ring off.'

'All right. But I want you to call tomorrow.'

'Okay, but I'm not sure at what time.'

'As long as you do,' he warned.

There was a long silence after she had rung off, and she twisted her hands together nervously. 'I'm sorry,' she said finally, not looking up.

'What did you say?' André ground out angrily.

'I—I can't say it again.'

'Then why say it at all? What the hell are you apologising for? The fact that you so nearly gave yourself to me, the fact that your boy-friend interrupted, or the fact that it happened at all?'

'I—I don't know!' she cried in anguish. 'It was so unlike anything that's ever happened to me before.'

'Oh yes? Then why was Matt giving you the third degree just now?' he demanded bitterly. 'It couldn't possibly be because he was jealous as hell, now could it?'

She shook her head. 'No—no, of course it couldn't. I told you that our relationship wasn't—*isn't* like that.'

André slammed down his glass. 'Then what was all that rubbish about my losing something? If you aren't having an affair with Matt what's to stop you——'

'Sleeping with you?' she finished for him. 'I've already told you that I'm not like that. I don't want that sort of relationship with anyone.'

'And yet if the telephone hadn't rung there's no knowing what would have happened,' he told her grimly.

'I like to think I would have been able to stop in time.' She blushed in her confusion.

'You like to think be damned!' He strode angrily to the door. 'Don't forget to feed the kitten and make sure she's warm. I'm going to bed—the company down here is too pure for my tainted body.'

'Oh, André, I didn't——'

'Go to bed, Caroline. And forget what happened.'

Forget it—how could she forget it? She tidied away the dirty dishes, washing them and putting them away in the cupboards, all the time sobbing uncontrollably. She fed the tiny kitten and carried it up to the warmth of her bedroom, placing its box before the fire. It looked so warm and comfortable and innocent. Innocent! That was something she felt she would never be again. She fell asleep with the feel of passionate lips and hands on her body and the knowledge that André Gregory could arouse in her passions she hadn't known she possessed.

CHAPTER FOUR

IT was already late in the morning when Caroline began to rouse, and then it was only the forlorn wail of the kitten that finally broke through the fog of her brain. Her sleep hadn't been restful and she had tossed and turned until the early hours of the morning when she had finally fallen into an exhausted slumber.

She leant over the side of the bed to find huge blue eyes fixed mournfully on her face. 'What's the matter, my pet?' she crooned. 'Are you hungry?' She threw back the bedclothes and getting out of bed padded over to the chair to pick up her wrap.

Picking up the kitten, she carried her down the stairs. It wasn't until Susi was tucking hungrily into a plateful of food that she noticed how quiet it was. The cottage was shrouded in silence. Where was André? She felt panic rise up inside her and rushing into the lounge she began a frantic search of the cottage. André was nowhere to be found.

She ran to the door to reassure herself that his car was still in the driveway. It wasn't! Oh God! He surely hadn't left without seeing her first. The thought was curiously painful, and she found herself wondering just how much she had come to depend on his company during the last few days.

He couldn't have gone! He just couldn't. Not after last night. But he had told her to forget what happened between them last night. Impossible. She would never forget those arousing kisses or the touch of his strong hands on her body. She blushed at the memory of her complete abandon, her surrender to her senses. If her father hadn't telephoned where would she be now? More to the point, where would André be? She had no doubt that wherever they would have been it would have been together. But where was he now?

She walked slowly back up the stairs, her thoughts racing wildly. If André had left surely he would have left a message for her. Of course he would. He must have just gone out for the day—after all, she didn't have any right to know where he had gone. She didn't own him.

She dialled her father's telephone number with shaking hands. 'Daddy?' she asked huskily.

'Caroline! You know I don't like you calling me at the office.'

'I'm sorry, Daddy. I—I just wondered if you'd heard from André?'

'Now why on earth should I hear from him? He's a big boy now, he doesn't ask for permission to move. What's the matter? Aren't the two of you talking to each other?'

'I don't know, Daddy. He's disappeared.'

'What do you mean, disappeared? Have the two of you had an argument?

Caroline blushed. 'Not—not exactly.'

'What does that mean? Either you have or you haven't. Did something happen last night that I should know about?'

Hardly! What had happened between André and herself was completely private. 'No—no, but I can't seem to find him anywhere. I thought perhaps he might have contacted you.' How weak that sounded! Why on earth should André contact her father, especially as he thought their relationship something it certainly wasn't.

'Well, surely the poor man doesn't have to report back to you when he goes out? He's there to rest, not humour a young girl. He's probably gone out for the day.'

'Without telling me?' The words were out before

she had time to think what interpretation her father might put on them.

'Caroline, André is my guest, and he has a perfect right to go just wherever he pleases.'

'I know, Daddy, but I——'

'Caroline! Leave the man alone, for goodness' sake. I'm sure nothing has happened to him. And if you wanted to go out for the day would you tell him?'

'Well, no, but I——'

'You see!' he interrupted. 'Now stop panicking. You were behaving strangely on the telephone last night. What was going on when I called you?'

'Nothing,' she lied. 'We'd just finished dinner and——' she broke off guiltily.

'And?' prompted her father.

'And after you telephoned I went to bed.'

'Alone?'

'Of course alone! What do you take me for?'

He sighed. 'My daughter. And I know that if you decided André was the man for you a little thing like the lack of a wedding ring wouldn't worry you.'

'Daddy!'

'Stop sounding so shocked, Caroline. You're a big girl now and I'm quite expecting you to suddenly produce a lover. So why not André?'

'Because I don't like him!' The words were spoken without thought, and her eyes widened with shock. It wasn't true any more, she didn't hate him at all. How could she when she had responded to him so ardently the evening before? 'Well, not much,' she amended huskily. 'And I won't be producing a lover, ever!'

'I think I must know you better than you know yourself. You're like your mother, loving and generous-natured.'

Caroline hadn't known her mother as she had died giving life to her, but she knew her father had loved her very much, that he still did, and that was why he had never remarried. 'Thank you, Daddy.' She knew his words were a compliment.

'But you're also stubborn and obstinate,' he continued, 'like me. And let me tell you that the combination is quite explosive in one woman. I pity poor André. Why don't you come home and stop annoying the man? It can't be much fun for him with you trying to be alluring all the time.'

'I am not!'

'Explosive, or trying to be alluring?'

'Either. I'm not using those sort of tactics. I'm only trying to be nice to him.'

'Caroline!'

'But I am. I——' she broke off as she heard the closing of the back door. 'Look, Daddy, I think André just came home. I have to go now.'

'But, Caroline——'

She didn't wait to hear any more but slammed down the telephone and ran down into the hallway. André had just entered the cottage and was brushing raindrops from his glistening dark hair. He stopped his movements as he saw her, his eyes narrowing as he looked at her. Caroline blushed under that unblinking stare, looking down awkwardly at her bare feet.

'Good morning,' he said coolly, removing his thick sheepskin jacket to throw it casually over the hall table. 'It's lousy out,' he remarked with a grimace.

She had been worrying herself silly about him and he came in and made comments about the weather! 'Where have you been?' she demanded angrily. 'How dare you go out and leave me here without telling me where you're going or when you'll be back?'

André's eyes became like green pebbles and his mouth a thin straight line. 'Forgive me if I'm wrong,' he said, dangerously soft, 'but I wasn't aware that I'd given you the right to question my movements. Have I?'

His voice gave the impression of icicles and Caroline shivered involuntarily. 'Well, no, but I——'

'Have I, Caroline?' he repeated harshly.

She shook her head miserably. 'No.'

'I thought not. Don't ever speak to me like that again. I don't know what sort of liberties you take with Matt, but I have no intention of allowing you to walk all over me. No doubt he enjoys it. I don't.'

'I wouldn't put the two of you in the same category,' she said sharply.

'Thank God for that! Caroline, are you going to get yourself dressed or is this another invitation?' he taunted.

'Another one?' Her cheeks were fiery red.

'Mm, another one. That's what last night was all about, wasn't it? What's the matter with you? Can't you do without a man for a few days?'

'W—what do you mean?'

'Surely it's obvious,' he ran his hand through his damp hair. 'Men play a very important part in your life, don't they? And I mean that in the plural. Matt doesn't strike me as the type of man capable of coping with someone of your appetites.'

'You're disgusting!' she snapped.

André smiled sneeringly. 'Because I have you worked out? Don't be stupid, Caroline. I'm to be used as a substitute, aren't I? Or maybe even a replacement. After all, Matt isn't getting any younger, is he? Play your cards right with me and maybe I'll take over your expensive upkeep, isn't that your idea?'

'No, it is not!' She stared at him wide-eyed with shock. 'I never thought of such a thing. All I was going to do was——'

'Get me hooked,' he finished dryly. 'And believe me, that wouldn't be too difficult. I find myself responding to you against my will.'

'That's some admission—from someone like you,' she added nastily.

'You're damned right it is! But it isn't going to work, not now, not ever. I'm too cynical about your sex to be taken in by your little game.'

'So last night meant nothing to you? You were just playing me along, weren't you?'

'And if I were?'

Caroline marched past him, intending to go up the stairs and get dressed. She only got as far as the second step when a firm grip on her arm brought her to an abrupt halt. 'Take your hands off me,' she said with remarkable calm.

'Not until you've answered my question.'

'All right!' she turned on him. 'If you were playing with me then you were very cruel.'

'So I'm cruel,' he dismissed with a shrug of his broad shoulders. 'I suppose what I'm about to tell you will also seem cruel.'

Her look sharpened. 'What's happened?'

André gave a mocking smile, moving away from her to remove his damp sweater and reveal the brown shirt he wore beneath it. 'Why do women always jump to the conclusion that something has "happened"?'

'So what did happen?'

'The kitten's owner is what happened.'

'Susi? You found her owner?'

He nodded. 'I enquired locally and found that six kittens had been born about four weeks ago at a farm down the road. One went missing early yesterday morning. They've been looking for it ever since.'

'Oh,' Caroline slumped down on the stairs. 'So they want Susi back.'

'Yes. The little girl has apparently been very upset. They have homes for the other five, but Susi was promised to the little girl who lives there.'

'I see. I suppose that pleases you, that you can take Susi away from me?'

'Don't be so damned childish! I looked for her home because it was only logical that she must have one. Debbie, the child, was overjoyed to think we might have found her. I'm sure you won't feel so bad about giving Susi back once you've seen her.'

'Thank you,' she said stiffly. 'I'm sure you're right, you're the sort of person who always is.'

'Oh hell! Grow up, Caroline! Why should one little kitten mean so much to you? Ask Matt, I'm sure he'll give you another one.'

'It isn't only the kitten,' she told him quietly. 'You could have taken me with you instead of sneaking off behind my back in that way.'

'I didn't *sneak* anywhere,' he said with controlled violence.

'Oh yes, you did. I'm not stupid, I knew I couldn't take the kitten back to my flat with me. I intended doing exactly what you've done this morning. But you had to go ahead behind my back, as if I'm a child or something.'

André sighed. 'I left early this morning because I couldn't sleep. I needed to think. The idea to look for the kitten's owner occurred to me when I was already out.'

'Oh yes?'

'Yes,' he answered impatiently. 'I don't have to prove anything to you, Caroline. What I do, and when I do it, is none of your affair. I told them we would take the kitten back this afternoon, you can please yourself whether you come or not.'

'Oh, I'm coming,' she told him firmly. 'I want Susi to go back to her family as much as you do.'

'Good. Now for God's sake go and put some clothes on and stop flaunting your body! Nearly every time

I see you you're only half dressed.' He looked at her with contempt.

'Certainly not to attract you!' she denied vehemently 'I don't even like you.'

'No one asked that you should. I don't require that you like me in order that I can get through the day.'

'What do you do for a living, Mr Gregory?' she sneered. 'I can't imagine you endear many people to you with your arrogant contempt of people.'

'I'm a business man, and doing very nicely, thank you,' he told her with a smile. 'People require integrity, not social pleasantries.'

'I wouldn't have credited you with that either,' came her parting shot as she ran up the stairs and into her bedroom. She had wanted to anger him, but knew by the half smile on those mocking lips that she had only succeeded in amusing him.

She sat down dejectedly on her unmade bed. The trouble was, she had never met anyone quite like André Gregory before, and she didn't know how to handle him. Her father was right, she was treading on dangerous ground trying to teach him a lesson. But she wouldn't give in; she had as much right to be here as he did, more if he only knew it. But his attitude only made her all the more determined that he shouldn't know she was Matt Rayner's daughter.

She spent the morning in her studio, refusing André's offer to get her lunch and making a sandwich for herself later. He made no comment at her definite snub, but continued to read his book unconcernedly.

Finally he stood up. 'Are you ready to leave?'

Caroline looked down at the sleeping bundle in her lap, absently stroking the soft black fur. 'I suppose so,' she said resentfully.

André took the kitten so she could stand up, placing it gently in the box she had made up. 'You don't have to come, Caroline. The kitten will be all right with me.'

'I know that. I may not like you very much, but I don't think you would be deliberately cruel to a defenceless animal. I'd like to come. Do you mind?'

'No,' he said shortly

'Well, don't sound so enthusiastic!'

It was only a short drive to the farm and André's powerful car covered the distance in a matter of minutes. He helped her out of the car by opening the door for her, leading the way to the door of the low rambling farmhouse. Caroline was glad she had thought to put on her rubber boots and tuck her denims into them at the knees. The yard was full of mud from the recent rain and she sloshed along behind André as he carried Susi.

The door was opened by a tall girl, her long black hair tied back away from her face. If Caroline had been expecting the epitome of a farmer's wife, make-upless face, wrapover floral pinafore, and scraped-back hair in an unbecoming bun, she was to be sadly disappointed. This woman was quite startlingly beautiful, her hair perfectly groomed back away from her face, her make-up flawless, and her dress impeccable. She was tall and confident, and her blue eyes brightened with recognition as she looked at André.

'Mr Gregory!' she greeted, opening the pine door for them to enter. The inside of the farmhouse was even more startling—pine furniture, deep pile carpets, and a dark brown leather three-piece suite. Not at all what Caroline had expected from the outside. It made her cottage look very poor in comparison. The woman took the box containing the kitten. 'Debbie will be so pleased. I can't tell you how grateful we all are.' At last she seemed to notice Caroline. 'Forgive me,' she smiled. 'My name is Eve Gresham.'

'And I'm——'

'Eve!' a male voice called, before a man of about thirty came hurriedly into the room. 'Ah, Mr Gregory, I thought it was your car.'

Eve Gresham smiled at the newcomer. 'And he's brought his wife with him this time too.'

'Oh, but I'm not!' burst out Caroline. 'André and I aren't *married*!'

The young man looked at André and then back to Caroline. 'But we thought—Mr Gregory said you were staying at the Rayner cottage just down the road. Both of you.'

Caroline nodded. 'That's right. We are.'

The man's skin coloured a ruddy hue and he began to look uncomfortable. 'I see,' he muttered awkwardly.

'I don't think you do,' at last André spoke. 'We're sharing the cottage, but that's all we're doing. We'd never met until a couple of days ago. We're both guests of the Rayner family. It was unfortunate that we both decided to come here at the same time, but completely unplanned, let me assure you.'

'Oh,' the other man smiled uncertainly. 'Well, I'm pleased to meet you. My name is Brian Wells,' and he put out his hand to her formally.

Caroline frowned her puzzlement. She was sure this woman's name was Gresham. 'Caroline—Rawlings,' the last came out awkwardly.

'My sister tells me that we have you to thank for finding the kitten,' he smiled at her. 'I can't tell you how grateful we are—Debbie's been so upset.'

His sister! Eve Gresham was his sister; that explained a lot. And she was very beautiful. Caroline looked suspiciously at André, only to find him looking at her with those compelling green eyes of his, his amusement at her expense evident by the mockery she could read there. She looked away in disgust. 'I can understand that,' she said huskily.

Brian Wells looked at her with unconcealed admiration, his blue eyes passing appreciatively over her slender body. He was quite young, in his early thirties at most, she would have said, with fair waving hair, a tanned complexion from working outside so much, and a tall loose-limbed body. He was handsome in an outdoor sort of way, and Caroline brightened under his intent stare.

'Would you like to come with me now and we can return the kitten to its mother?' he smiled at her. 'Debbie's probably already out there, she calls in there first every day on her way home from school.'

'I would love to.'

She was conscious of those mocking green eyes following her as she left the room and her head rose haughtily. The barn they entered several minutes later was warm and sheltered, a big pile of straw in one corner providing a home for the black cat and her five kittens, six once they had placed Susi back among her brothers and sisters.

A little girl of about six looked up at them as they crouched down to watch the antics of the young kittens. She had the long dark hair of Eve Gresham, and also the promise of her beauty in her clear blue eyes and peachy complexion.

'Uncle Brian,' she exclaimed happily, watching the greeting between Susi and her mother. 'You've brought Bobby back for me!'

Caroline couldn't resist a smile. She had even got the sex of the kitten wrong! The excitement in the little girl's face was all she needed to help her over the feeling of loss at bringing back the kitten.

'Miss Rawlings here found your kitten, Debbie,' Brian Wells explained. 'Aren't you going to thank her?'

'Oh yes,' Debbie smiled shyly. 'Thank you, Miss Rawlings.'

'I think you can call me Caroline,' she smiled.

'Run along to the house now, Debbie,' her uncle

told her. 'Tell Mummy we'll be over to the house in a moment.'

The little girl went off quite happily once she had seen Susi/Bobby settled. Caroline watched her go. 'She's very like her mother,' she commented idly.

'Very,' Brian agreed. 'My sister is a widow,' he explained. 'Her husband was killed when Debbie was only two. I'm afraid Eve often becomes bored here, although Debbie loves it.'

Caroline had wondered about *Mr* Gresham, now she had had her curiosity answered. No wonder André Gregory had been eager to come back here this afternoon; he was obviously interested in the young widowed Mrs Gresham. 'It's a wonderful place for a child to grow up,' she said finally.

'That's what we think,' he replied thoughtfully. 'Otherwise Eve would probably have moved into a town. Still, you don't want to hear about us. Are you here on holiday?'

'Sort of.'

'And Mr Gregory?'

'The same, I think.' She didn't really know a lot about the man, only that he knew her father well enough to be invited to stay at the cottage. Her father hadn't been very forthcoming about him, and she was usually too angry to bother to ask personal questions.

'I see.' He shifted uncomfortably. 'And you aren't here—well, together?'

She gave a very definite shake of her head. 'No!'

He smiled shyly. 'In that case, I don't suppose you would care to come out to dinner with me some time? There's a good inn about three miles away where they serve the best grills I've ever tasted.'

'The Three Horseshoes? I've been there once before, with—with a friend.' She had been going to say her father, and then thought better of it. Better to keep this pretence going with everyone; André

Gregory would learn of his mistake soon enough. 'And I agree with you, they *do* serve delicious meals.'

'Then you'll come?' he asked eagerly.

'I'd love it,' she accepted gratefully. He seemed to be a nice man, and anyway, she needed a break from André Gregory's taunts.

'Tonight?'

She nodded. 'If you like.'

'That's great. Eight o'clock all right?'

'Lovely.'

She noted the becoming flush to Eve Gresham's cheeks and the look of satisfaction on André Gregory's face when they returned to the house. She drank the cup of tea with barely concealed impatience. It was made all the worse because she didn't understand her feelings. Why should she feel annoyed because Eve Gresham felt attracted to André? Why should it matter to her one way or the other? Her father had told her she had no right to expect anything from him, and he was right, not even if André had almost made love to her the night before!

'You're very quiet,' André commented on the drive back to the cottage. 'Anything wrong?'

'No, nothing,' she answered primly.

He smiled mockingly. 'It sounds like it! What's the matter, didn't you like our neighbours?'

'I thought they were very nice,' she said stiffly.

The hand nearest her left the steering wheel, moving to wrench her chin round until she was looking at him, anger at his treatment of her burning in her brilliant blue eyes. 'You thought they were nice,' he repeated softly. 'Then why were you so eager to leave?'

'I wasn't!' she denied heatedly.

He held her chin firmly in his hand. 'Yes, you were. Jealous, Caro?'

Her eyes blazed and she tried to wrench out of his grasp—and failed miserably. He had a strength that was unshakeable. The fight died out of her and she sat back with deceptive calm. André relinquished his hold on her chin, running caressing fingers over her parted lips. It was just the opportunity she had been waiting for, opening her mouth and sinking her teeth painfully into his finger.

He quickly pulled his hand away, not by a flicker of emotion showing the pain she must have inflicted, but his eyes darkened ominously. 'You little bitch!' His gaze remained fixed on the road. 'You'll pay for that.'

'Promises, promises,' she taunted.

He looked at her fleetingly. 'That's no promise,' he said grimly. 'That's a threat, and one I mean to carry out.'

'That really frightens me, Mr Gregory. You don't know how much.' Brave words, but she did feel a little nervous of him. She had acted impulsively once again. Her father had always told her it would get her into trouble one day, and she had the feeling that day was very near.

André Gregory was like no other man she had ever met; he was older for one thing, much more mature, and fully conscious of his own attraction. He had a self-assurance that bordered on arrogance, and he exuded a sensuous aura that attracted her while frightening her. It was a strange admission for her to make; she had always been the one in control, always managed to get her own way with her male acquaintances. And yet André Gregory reduced her coolness to burning anger and her body to pure desire. She had never felt as she had last night with any man before, and for a short space of time she had been at his mercy, with no mind of her own.

'I'm glad about that,' he said softly. 'Because I mean it.'

'So you said.'

She didn't wait for him to get out of the car but walked into the cottage without him. It seemed curiously quiet without the kitten, and she realised their only polite source of conversation had been removed in Susi. They would probably resort to verbal abuse when talking to each other now. Who was she kidding? They had never done anything else. André had admitted that last night had merely been an experiment on his part, to prove to her that he could use her and forget her. And he had almost succeeded!

'Don't wait dinner for me,' she said carelessly. 'I'm going out this evening.'

'Brian Wells?'

'Jealous, André?' she asked with sugary sweetness.

His eyes swept over her scathingly, stripping every piece of clothing from her body. 'Hardly,' he said dryly. 'I'm going out myself, as it happens.'

'I won't ask with who, I can make a good guess.'

'You'd be wrong. Who would baby-sit?' he taunted.

'So you're going to the Wells farm for the evening? Oh well, at least you'll have complete privacy that way.'

'You have a sharp little tongue, Caroline, and you aren't very complimentary about Eve Gresham's morals. I'm quite aware of your opinion of me, but surely you have no reason to be rude about her? I'm sure she's done nothing to warrant such accusations.'

'Oh no, except fawn all over you. She made a positive fool of herself.'

'Something you would never do, would you, Caroline? That cool little head of yours works everything out logically, doesn't it? Like your relationship with Matt—you can't really love him, in fact I know you don't. You couldn't have reacted to me as you did when you love another man.'

She faced him defiantly. 'I love him very much,' she declared. 'And it would take more than physical excitement to change that,' and it would; no matter whom she met she would always love her father.

André took a step towards her, noting her involuntary step backwards with mocking humour. 'That isn't real fear I see in your eyes, it's fear of what I can do to you. And in the right circumstances I can do quite a lot, can't I?'

'You're disgusting! I'm glad I'm going out tonight. Why don't you go and inflict your company on someone else?'

He gave a bored yawn. 'You could always leave. No one's forcing you to stay here with me. I would welcome the privacy.'

'I'm sure you would, now that you've found someone who's impressed by your damned arrogance. But I'm not going anywhere, I have the right to be here. Excuse me, I have to shower and change.'

'Be my guest,' he taunted.

Her eyes flashed. 'I am not *your* guest!'

André grinned at her. 'Just a figure of speech.'

'I'll bet.' She ran up the stairs, slamming the bedroom door hard behind her. The audacity of the man! Well, she pitied poor Eve Gresham, having to put up with the conceit of the man. She banged about in her room, opening drawers and cupboards as she looked for clothing to wear tonight. How dared he talk to her like that, taunting her with her desire for him as if she was completely permissive. How dared he!

She sat down suddenly, clasping the silk blouse against her. Who was she trying to kid? She was jealous as hell of the evening he would be spending with the other woman. Oh, not because she especially liked him, but because tonight he would probably be with Eve Gresham as he had been with her last night— and not caring that it was a different woman! That was part of the reason she despised him. He didn't see her as a person in her own right, only as an object, an object used for desire and nothing else.

Oh, damn the man! Why should she care what he thought, he wasn't important to her. She would go out this evening and enjoy herself. Brian Wells was young and good-looking and there was positively no reason why they shouldn't enjoy their evening together.

Brian Wells was the exact opposite of André, in looks as well as in character. The younger man was blond, with fair colouring, laughing blue eyes, and not an ounce of the arrogance in his nature that made André such a formidable opponent. Brian was clear-cut and uncomplicated, something she needed after a couple of days in André's company.

She stayed in her room until she heard the two men talking together downstairs on Brian's arrival. She took a last glance in the mirror to assure herself she was looking her best. She had chosen to wear a below-the-knee russet-coloured dress, loose-fitting but gathered in at her narrow waist, long sleeved, and a roll-neck that gave her the look of a chaste nun, and when combined with her knee-length boots it allowed none of her body below the neck to be visible. She didn't want to be too overdressed for the inn they were going to, having learnt from previous visits that the patrons of the inn wore casual clothing, often only denims and tee-shirts. But she had wanted to wear something smarter than that, if only to show André Gregory that she was looking forward to her evening out with Brian.

The two men were in the lounge when she came downstairs, both of them standing up politely as she entered the room. Brian looked very smart, in a navy blazer, a lighter blue shirt, combined with grey trousers, but it was André who made the most impression on her senses. His black shirt was opened down to the waist, showing his deeply tanned chest and the dark hairs growing there, and Caroline looked hurriedly away again as she saw him watching her reaction to him. And he had his shoes off again! Didn't he ever bother with manners? He had known Brian was coming here tonight, he could at least have made an effort to look presentable.

She glared at him resentfully before smiling at Brian. 'I hope I haven't kept you waiting,' she said softly.

He returned her smile. 'Not at all. And even if you had I believe you would have been worth waiting for. Wouldn't you agree, Mr Gregory?'

'André, please. I think Caro's worth waiting for at any time,' he answered smoothly.

Brian frowned his puzzlement. 'Caro?' he questioned.

André shrugged. 'Just my name for her.'

'Oh. I—I see,' he turned to look at her. 'Well, if you're ready to leave ...'

Caroline held herself aloof, resenting André's implied intimacy between the two of them. 'I'm ready,' she told him between gritted teeth.

André came to stand behind her as she gathered up her handbag. 'Have fun, children,' he murmured for her ears alone. 'And don't do anything I wouldn't, Caro.'

She turned angrily to face him. 'That means I can do just about anything!' she retorted hotly.

He nodded. 'Just about. Would you like me to wait up for you?' he taunted.

'Get lost!' she muttered. 'Daddykins!' she added bitchily.

'But not yours, and certainly not your *sugar*-daddy.'

'Do you always have to have the last word?'

'With you—yes.'

'Oh, go away!'

'I'll wait up for you—just to make sure you get home all right. You never know, he may turn violent.'

She glanced hurriedly at Brian, conscious of his

puzzled looks in their direction. 'Don't be ridiculous! And don't bother waiting up for me—I may be late, very late.'

'I'll wait anyway,' came the quiet reply.

CHAPTER FIVE

CAROLINE'S anger lasted all the way to the inn, when she finally realised she wasn't being fair to Brian. It wasn't his fault André kept annoying her.

'It's pleasant here, isn't it?' she remarked as they sat down at a table in the corner of the room. Small red lamps shone on each individual table, allowing the occupants a clear vision of their companions only, and leaving the rest of the room in shadow.

'Very pleasant,' he agreed readily. 'But not exactly what you're used to, I should imagine.'

'Sorry?' she frowned her puzzlement.

'You live in London, don't you?' he said jerkily. 'We aren't exactly up to that standard.'

'Are you annoyed about something, Brian?' she guessed shrewdly.

He moved nervously. 'Well, I—I didn't like that man's familiarity!' he said in a rush. 'You both say there's nothing between the two of you and yet he—he—well, he seems *possessive* of you.'

Caroline looked astounded. 'I'm sure you're wrong, Brian. I've only known him a couple of days, and we don't exactly get on together.'

'That wasn't the impression he gave me.'

Her look sharpened. 'Did he say something to you?'

'He implied that you've had some sort of lover's tiff,' he told her stiffly.

'I'm sure you're wrong,' she shook her head dazedly. 'You must have misunderstood him—André wouldn't say something like that, there's no foundation for it.'

'Well, if you say so,' he accepted reluctantly. 'Let's order our meal, shall we?'

Caroline was eager to comply, wanting desperately to put all thought of that hateful man completely out of her mind for the rest of the evening. She wanted to put an end to this charade, tell him exactly who she was and watch him squirm. But he hadn't gone far enough yet, hadn't made enough disparaging remarks about 'Cynthia' Rayner. But when the time came she would make him pay for every slight against her, every little insult and insinuation. Then they would see who was so damned sure of themselves!

Brian turned out to be just as good a companion as she had imagined, and the evening passed quickly in relaxing enjoyment. Her mixed grill was perfect and the wine chilled as she liked it.

The two of them sat in the lounge-bar later in the evening the cheery fire adding extra warmth to the centrally heated room. Caroline sat back with a sigh. She hadn't realised how tense she had become in the past few days, and it was nice to be with someone she could just relax with.

'I've enjoyed myself this evening,' she smiled her pleasure.

Brian smiled back bashfully. 'So have I. We must do it again some time.'

Caroline frowned. 'I'm not really sure how much longer I shall be staying at the cottage.'

'I suppose Mr Gregory's presence there rather limits your activities,' he suggested.

'Not really,' she pursed her lips thoughtfully. 'I hadn't actually intended staying this long when I came down here. Now my plans are undecided. I'm just living from day to day. I enjoy being here.'

'I believe I may have seen you about these parts before, now I come to think about it. I was working up on one of the top fields during the summer, August I think it was, and I'm sure I saw you with Mr Rayner, travelling in a blue sports car.'

'I suppose it could have been me.' She was reluctant to reveal too much—Brian might put two and two together, and being unbiased, unlike André Gregory, he just might come up with the right answer. 'I do have a sports car, and I was here during the summer.'

'I know it was definitely Mr Rayner,' Brian continued. 'I've met him a couple of times.'

'It was probably me with him, then,' she admitted. 'Do you come to this restaurant often?' she asked, anxious to change the subject.

Their conversation became more general after this, and the time passed so swiftly that Caroline looked at her watch in surprise when they rang the bell for closing time. Brian had been an undemanding companion, shyly revealing a little of his background and the hard work that was finally beginning to pay off. Ten years of pure hard work had gone into making him the moderately successful farmer he was today, but he sounded as if it had all been worth it.

'It's a hard life for a woman,' he remarked on the journey back to her cottage. 'I'll never know how Eve always manages to look so cool and composed.'

It was something that Caroline had wondered about too. The woman's perfectly groomed appearance earlier today seemed to be a daily thing rather than a chance occurrence. She felt sure that in similar circumstances, caring for a young child and a farmhouse, besides the farmer, she would not appear so immaculate. 'She must enjoy it.'

'Up to a point. But she's still young and there aren't too many eligible men for her to meet around here.'

Caroline felt like pointing out that she had just met one in André, a very eligible male at that, although she couldn't imagine Brian being too pleased about having André as a brother-in-law. But then she couldn't imagine him married; 'love them and leave them' appeared to be his motto.

'She seemed happy enough,' she pointed out.

'Oh, she is, don't get me wrong, but it's mainly because living here makes Debbie happy.' He turned to look at her in the darkness of the car. 'Will you come out with me again?'

'I would love to.' She hadn't missed the bright light still shining in the sitting-room of the cottage. If André had dared to wait up for her——!

'Tomorrow?' he persisted.

'Well .... maybe not tomorrow.' She liked him, but not enough for him to want to think seriously about her. 'Perhaps the day after?'

'Fine. We could go out for a drink somewhere.'

'Right,' she agreed. 'Call me, hmm?'

By the time she entered the cottage a few minutes later she was furiously angry. She burst into the sitting-room, her eyes going straight to André as he stood by the curtained window. She threw her handbag down into one of the chairs. 'Just what the hell do you think you're doing?'

He raised a mocking eyebrow at her outburst, holding up the half empty glass in his hand. 'Helping myself to Matt's whisky. I would have thought it was obvious.'

'Don't be patronising!' she snapped. 'You were spying on me,' she accused.

André moved forward into the room. 'Watching to see if there were any fond farewells, you mean? Do I look like a voyeur?'

'I didn't mean——'

'The chaste little kisses you can be expected to share with Brian Wells can hardly be called good viewing,' he taunted, throwing back his head and tipping a liberal amount of the fluid to the back of his throat.

'Why should they be expected to be chaste little kisses?' she demanded indignantly.

He shrugged. 'What else could they be? Brian Wells

is what's known as a "nice" man. He wouldn't take advantage of your generous nature. Besides, Caro, he isn't half man enough for you.'

'And I suppose you are?' she scoffed.

'Oh, assuredly. I could handle you quite easily. But I'm not going to.'

'You won't get the chance!'

'*Second* chance, you mean.'

'Second——? Oh!' she blushed. 'You're disgusting!'

André put the glass down on the table, flexing his shoulder muscles. 'You're quite exciting when you're angry, Caro. In fact, very exciting.'

She visibly moved away from the darkening sensuality in his eyes. 'Leave me alone,' she ordered. 'Not content with—with spying on me out of the window— oh no, you now decide that you have to prove how strong, how virile you are!'

André didn't appear at all concerned by her tirade, in fact, by the throaty chuckle he was giving she would say he was very amused, at her expense. 'I don't have to prove anything, Caro. You seem to be the one who has to prove something. What's the matter? Is Matt cooling in his attentions?'

'Will you stop these stupid accusations about—about my—about Mr Rayner!' She inwardly groaned, wishing now that she could stop this farce, explain to him just who she was. But a lingering desire for revenge forced her to remain silent, holding out for the ultimate effect on this mocking, taunting, *arrogant* man. 'They're completely untrue.'

'You think so?' he shrugged, picking up the burgundy-coloured leather jerkin that lay across the table. 'Well, if you like to delude yourself into thinking that everything between you and Matt is innocently romantic, who am I to argue with you? I suppose this way you can excuse your behaviour to your friend.'

There was a definite sneer to his voice now, and what had started out as just barbed teasing was fast becoming another slanging match.

'My behaviour doesn't need excusing, but yours could use some looking at,' she said crossly.

'Surely your friend doesn't approve of you having an affair with her father? There can't be much difference in your ages,' he added with disgust.

'There isn't any! And as our only polite source of conversation has been removed in Susi, I think I'll go to bed before you insult me any more!' She turned on her heel.

'You do that,' came the quiet taunt from close behind her. 'I think I'll join you.'

'You most certainly will not!' She turned on him angrily. 'Just what do you take me for!'

'I haven't worked out yet what category you fit into,' he admitted with a grin. 'But give me time, I will. And when I said I was going to bed too, I didn't mean yours.'

'Oh,' Caroline blushed at her mistake. 'I see.'

He passed her to take the stairs two at a time. 'You have a very inflated opinion of your effect on men,' he said shortly. 'And while I admit you're very beautiful, that doesn't mean that every man you meet wants to jump into bed with you. Now you can safely go off to bed without fearing I may rush into your bedroom in the middle of the night to slake my heated passions upon your body.'

'Don't talk to me as if I'm an imaginative child!'

'Then don't act like one.' His eyes had darkened, this time with anger. 'Goodnight!' and he slammed his bedroom door behind him.

'Goodnight . . . .'

Her sketching wasn't going well, even though this room was ideal for her purposes; once being a loft bedroom it now served very well as a studio. No, it wasn't her surroundings that were obstructive to her work, it was her thoughts that held her back. Her mind wasn't on what she was doing, but on André Gregory, and each time she began her preliminary sketches it was his face that looked back at her. She ripped out her latest effort, throwing it angrily on the floor with the other ten she had started this morning.

Why *did* that man keep haunting her thoughts? It was partly because he was such a strong personality, she knew that. He had a way of making his presence felt without speaking a single word, which was how their breakfast had progressed this morning. She had pointedly ignored him, going out of her way to show him her displeasure, while he happily read the newspaper he had been out to collect.

Now he had gone out again without a word to her, and she still couldn't get him out of her mind. She looked down at her twelfth attempt, only to find that arrogant face staring back at her once again. She threw the pencil and pad down on the floor at her side, lying back on the couch with her feet on the arm at the other end.

Where had he gone? Was he thinking of her as she couldn't stop thinking of him? She doubted it. He was a mystery man, seemingly a prosperous business man, and yet she had never heard of him. Just who was André Gregory? And why had she never heard him mentioned by any of her friends, or by her father for that matter?

She picked up her sketch pad, pursing her lips as she studied the firm lines of his face—very strong and compelling, with a strength of purpose that made him walk over everything that stood in his way. And she was in his way. He had come here wanting solitude, and yet she irritatingly refused to leave.

A sudden thought occurred to her. Supposing he

had attempted to make love to her the other evening as a way of getting her to leave? If she were really Matt's girl-friend it was natural to assume she wouldn't want to stay here with another man and perhaps evoke Matt's anger. Unless of course she was after pastures greener, as André had suggested. And if she was as innocent as she insisted she was then she wouldn't want to stay here with a man who made no secret of the fact that he had desired her, been prepared to take her to his bed if the telephone hadn't interrupted them. Either way he had been more or less sure she would leave.

But she hadn't. She had the advantage over him of knowing that Matt was her father—not her lover, and that any time he pushed his attentions too far she could ask *him* to leave. She sighed. All this thought didn't tell her where he was—or who he was with. She wasn't even sure why she wanted to know.

'Caro? Caro!'

She jumped up eagerly as she heard her name being called. André! A smile lit up her face and she felt extraordinarily happy for some reason. She opened the studio door. 'Up here!' she called.

He entered the studio, looking about the room with interest. 'Mm, not bad,' he approved one of her earlier efforts that hung on the wall. 'Cynthia did that one, I suppose?' He sat on the arm of the couch looking at her.

'No. I—I did that one.' She had almost forgotten who Cynthia was supposed to be!

André raised one dark eyebrow. 'I see, allowed to hang your paintings here too. You're like an extra member of the family, aren't you? Why doesn't Matt marry you if you're that close?'

'He'll never marry me.' She tried to snatch her sketch pad out of his hand, but failed miserably.

For long seconds he continued to stare at the rough sketch of his dominant features. Finally he looked up. 'This is very good.' A certain amount of respect had entered his eyes. 'Have you had proper lessons?' he asked interestedly.

'Only at finishing school. I'm not good enough for anything else.'

He put down the pad. 'Well, I admit that you're never likely to make your living as a portrait painter, you're too brutally honest for that. People tend not to see themselves as they really are, and they don't want anyone to show it to them.'

'Because I've managed to show your arrogance with a few lines on paper?' she asked, stung into anger by his words.

'Something like that,' he agreed. 'Not that your drawing of me bothers me one way or the other. It's very good, you've caught me exactly.'

'That's what I thought. Did you want me for something?' she queried sweetly.

He moved the discarded sketches with his foot. 'I'm going fishing. I wondered if you would like to come along for the fresh air.' He bent to pick up a couple of the screwed-up pieces of paper, smoothing them out to look at them critically. 'Mm, I think you kept the best one.'

Caroline snatched the sketches out of his hand and ripped them in two. 'I didn't invite your interest.' She turned away. 'Surely you aren't going fishing this time of year?'

'Why not? The fish are still in there, no matter what time of year it is. Matt told me there's a lake about half a mile away.'

'There is—I just don't see you as the fishing type.'

'I'm not usually, but Matt said I could use his gear, see if I like it. I'll try anything once. I believe it's supposed to be restful.'

'So I've heard. My—Matt seems to have said quite a lot to you,' she said casually. 'I didn't realise you knew him that well.'

André stood up, flexing his muscles under the fitted black shirt. 'I've known him for years. Just because you're his girl-friend it doesn't mean he has to tell you about all his friends.'

That would have been true if that were the true circumstances of their relationship, but it seemed rather strange in the real state of facts. She must ask her father for further details about this man. It seemed strange that he hadn't telephoned today.

'Have you been abroad or something? That tan wasn't acquired here in England,' and it could explain her never having heard of him.

'I live in the States a lot of the time, and Australia too. I have business interests in both places. I've just spent three months in Australia. Answer your question?' he mocked.

'Yes.' She tidied the room, throwing away all the sketches of him, including the one in the pad. She avoided his taunting eyes.

'So how about you? You're not exactly one of the most talked-about women in the country.'

But she was! The gossip columns always seemed to be coupling her name with one man or another, and as she was expected to be one of the richest women in the world one day, they often speculated who was to be her consort. 'No,' she lied huskily.

'And Matt's kept pretty quiet about you too.'

'Wouldn't you?'

Those green eyes swept over her, noting the soft firm curves below the checked shirt and fitted denims she wore. 'I guess I would,' he eventually agreed. 'He probably doesn't want to take the risk of losing you.'

'He'll never lose me.' Fathers never lost their daughters.

'Okay. So are you coming fishing or aren't you?'

'Well, as you've never fished before I think I should come along and make sure you don't fall in or something. At least if that happens I can have a good laugh. I wouldn't like to miss that.'

'Thanks!'

She gave a grin. 'Now that I think about it I'm quite looking forward to it.'

André laughed too. 'Believe me, if I go in I'll make sure I take you with me, even if I have to get back out and carry you in.'

'That isn't very nice.'

'No,' he agreed with relish.

Caroline licked her lips nervously. 'Look, are you sure—I mean, are you sure you want me along? Last night——'

He shrugged. 'Last night was last night.'

'And this morning,' she added resentfully.

'Ah, now that was your fault.' He turned her forcefully out of the room and pushed her into her bedroom. She looked at him sharply. He sighed. 'My, my, you are suspicious! You'll need some warmer clothing on to go fishing, it's damned cold out there. Forget this morning,' he dismissed. 'You were just sulking.'

'I was not! I——'

'Caroline!' he warned impatiently. 'I'm not the most forgiving of men, but I'm willing to start again where you're concerned. If you don't want to do that then that's fine by me, I can get through life without us being friends.'

'I see, this offer to take me with you is in the nature of an olive branch?'

'If you like to think so.' He moved back to the door. 'You have five minutes to get ready. 'I'll be waiting in the car, I've already packed the fishing gear.'

'Do you want any lunch packed?' Caroline pulled

a thick sweater out of one of the drawers.

'I don't think so. Perhaps we can call in at a pub for lunch first. I don't particularly want to eat after handling maggots.'

She screwed up her face. 'Maggots! Can't you use something else? Da—Matt always uses sweet corn and cheese.'

'*Darling* Matt,' he guessed her unfinished word completely wrong, 'has some pretty good ideas at times. Did he catch anything worth getting cold for?'

'Quite a few large fish. I couldn't tell you the names of them, I'm not up on fish, I'm afraid.'

'Oh well, sweet corn and cheese will do. To tell you the truth, I didn't fancy touching maggots. I'm not even sure I'm going to like fishing.'

'But you'll try anything once,' she teased, not sure herself that he had the patience that seemed to be required for this pastime; her father usually packed up and came home after a couple of hours.

Five minutes later, the sweet corn and cheese duly added to the fishing gear, they were on their way. They decided to forgo lunch and have a big meal later. It wasn't far to the lake, but it could have seemed that way if they had had to carry all the paraphernalia that seemed to be necessary for what seemed a boring hobby to Caroline. She had only agreed to come because she was fed up with her own company.

She helped him unload the car and watched in amusement for the next ten minutes as he attempted to put the rod and line together. 'So, where did you go this morning?' she asked casually.

André looked at her sharply, but her face remained impassive, revealing none of the intense interest she really felt. She hadn't forgotten the explosion of yesterday morning to risk his anger again so quickly. 'I went to get this.' He took something out of his pocket and threw it at her.

'Caroline picked it up, turning it over. 'Oh,' she said disappointedly. 'A one-day fishing licence.'

'Where did you expect me to have been?' He grinned his satisfaction at the completion of his task.

She shrugged. 'I don't know.'

'I haven't been with Eve Gresham, if that's what you've been thinking. In fact, I haven't seen her since we called at the farm together yesterday.'

'But last night——'

'Last night I let you believe what you wanted to believe—and you certainly did that! I went out to dinner—alone. If you remember I did tell you I wasn't seeing Mrs Gresham. You didn't want to listen.'

'I just assumed ...'

'You just assumed that because Eve Gresham is a beautiful woman, and I like beautiful women, I would automatically make a play for her. It doesn't always work that way. I'm not saying I couldn't find her very attractive, I'm just saying she doesn't interest me at the moment. I don't like getting involved where children are concerned—so that rules you out completely,' he added tauntingly.

'André! You——'

'All right,' he held up a silencing hand. 'I was just teasing you. You're too sensitive. I couldn't give a damn about the seventeen years' difference in our ages. If you carry on gaining experience as you have been doing you'll soon catch me up anyway.'

'André! You said you wanted us to start again,' she reminded him.

'I'm not sure that's really possible. I still have too vivid a picture of how good you felt in my arms. Give me a few days and perhaps I'll get over it.'

Caroline lapsed into silence, not wishing to dissect her own reaction to him too deeply. She had avoided doing so ever since it happened, and Brian's kiss of last night had done little to wipe out the memory. That was probably why André's taunting had angered her so much. He happened to be right in everything he had said.

'Do you have to?' she asked suddenly.

'Have to what?' His concentration was all on the float bobbing happily on the water, waiting for that extra large bob that would tell him a fish was biting his bait.

'Get over it.' She avoided his probing eyes.

'Oh, I think so. If only out of loyalty to Matt. I take it you do know what loyalty is?'

'I know. And if I were to tell you——' she took a deep breath. 'If I were to tell you that there's nothing between Matt and myself, how would you feel then?'

'I would feel you were lying. I've witnessed his concern for you, remember?'

'And if I told you that was guilt, guilt because he wants to end things between us and is too nice a man to be able to tell me?'

'Then I would definitely know you were lying,' he said firmly. 'Matt isn't a fool, and if he didn't want you he would tell you honestly. Why should all this concern me anyway? There's been one incident between us that could be termed as not strictly innocent, everything else between us is the politeness that has to exist between two people attempting to share a house.'

Caroline's mouth tightened. She would get to this man if it was the last thing she did! He wasn't as indifferent to her as he kept insisting he was, and she intended to prove that to him. It was going to take time, that was all, but the feeling of elation at the end of it would be worth it.

As she had guessed, fishing didn't suit André; the couple of feeble bites he had did not excite his interest at all. Two hours after they had started out they were back in the car, the main catch of the day a large lump of weed from the bottom of the lake.

'Come on,' André turned to grin at her. 'I'll make you an extra large late lunch. This place isn't exactly overflowing with entertainment. What do you usually do when you come here? No—strike that question. It's pretty obvious what you do, in between sketching and painting, of course.'

'You're wrong. Matt hardly ever comes here. His daughter uses it much more than he does.'

'He didn't tell me that,' he frowned. 'It could have been rather awkward if it had been her here instead of you.'

They drew into the yard at the back of the cottage. 'Why any more awkward than us sharing?'

André opened the car door for her. 'Just think what the newspapers could make of it: "Famous business tycoon at girl's love-nest",' he quoted. 'I can just see it now,' he grimaced. 'And I wouldn't like it, believe me.'

Neither would she! She didn't mind playing this little game off against André in private, but she didn't want anyone else to know of their living arrangements. But someone else already knew, her father! And he wasn't past using his knowledge to get her to meet Greg Fortnum. She realised now that she had played right into his hands. No wonder he hadn't insisted too strongly on her leaving; this hold over her would suit him perfectly. The scandal, if this ever got out, wouldn't cause a ripple in her father's life, whereas it could absolutely ruin her own. The devious old devil!

But she couldn't wholly blame him for taking advantage of the accidental situation here; he had ordered her to return home. And she had refused, as he had known she would! She had never responded to direct orders, and he knew it—wily old fox!

André looked in at the open door at her. 'Are you going to sit there all day?' He locked the car door as she stepped out. 'And why the smile?'

She looked at him vaguely. 'Oh, just thoughts.'

'Pleasant ones, no doubt.'

'Just thoughts.'

'Well, come on, I'm going to make you the best beefburgers you've ever tasted—with all the trimmings,' he promised.

He was as good as his word, and Caroline could hardly move after eating just one of the gigantic beefburgers, topped with onions, lettuce, and tomato. André managed to eat two, but he looked just as ready to burst as she did when he had finished them.

When the telephone rang she naturally assumed it would be her father. She made a grab for the telephone, but André was there before her. 'It's for you,' he handed her the receiver. 'Wells,' he added.

'Brian!' her face brightened. 'What can I do for you?'

'Quite a lot, I should think,' came the cryptic comment from behind her.

She put her hand over the mouthpiece. 'Do you mind!' she glared at him.

'Just carry on, don't mind me.'

'I don't intend to.' She turned away. 'That sounds lovely, Brian. What time? Seven o'clock? That will be fine. Right, I'll see you tomorrow,' and she put down the telephone.

'My, my,' André taunted. 'You are popular today!'

Caroline put down her coffee cup. 'So are you, apparently. We're both invited over to dinner tomorrow evening. I accepted for both of us,' she gave him a sweet smile.

'I see,' he pursed his lips thoughtfully. 'Sometimes I wish the telephone had never been invented.'

'I'm sure Mrs Gresham would only have walked over and invited you if that were the case.'

'Maybe.' André lay back in the chair, his bare feet

resting on the mantelpiece. 'Mm, this is the relaxing life I need. I think I could get to quite like it if I stayed too long.'

Caroline looked at him sharply. 'You're thinking of leaving?'

'No, not yet anyway.'

'Oh.' She tried not to sound too happy about it, but she knew if he left now she wouldn't want to stay any longer either. The cottage would seem flat and lifeless without him here, his caustic tongue could be quite cutting at times, but he added the necessary spice to alleviate the boredom.

She watched him now as the firelight played across the fine planes of his face. A strong face that dominated, eyes like emeralds and as piercing as a jungle cat, firm white teeth, a strong jawline, all held at an arrogant angle. It was an arresting face, one not easily forgotten, and in the recesses of her mind she knew she had seen him somewhere before. Most of all it was a face worth getting down on canvàs.

'Would you sit for me?' She looked at him hopefully.

André ran a hand over his darkened jawline. 'You mean you want to paint me?' He quirked an eyebrow at her.

'That's the general idea,' she nodded.

'Why?'

'You have an interesting face,' she admitted grudgingly. 'Very striking.'

'And what would you do with the portrait once it was finished?'

Good question. In fact she had no idea what she would do with a painting of this man, she only knew she wanted to paint him. 'Perhaps you would like to have it?' she suggested.

'Buy it, you mean?'

'No,' she snapped. 'I don't sell my paintings, they aren't good enough for that. Anyway, I don't need the money.'

'And I don't really need a portrait of myself.'

'Oh, please yourself!' She stood up angrily.

He smiled at her anger. 'What a little spitfire you are! Don't be so touchy. If you want something to do then by all means paint me. But don't expect me to sit still for hours on end. You'll just have to make some sketches and work from those. I don't like being restricted—in any way.'

'I usually work that way anyway. I have a great one of Matt, would you like to see it?' she asked eagerly.

'If I must,' he said in a bored voice.

'Don't force yourself!'

'Oh, go and get it, girl. If you don't soon get used to my abrupt manner there are going to be a lot of arguments around here during the next few days.' He turned to look at her. 'Go and get the painting. Or would you rather I came up with you?'

As it hung in place of honour in her bedroom she didn't think that was a good idea. 'No. I I won't be a moment.'

It didn't take her long to run upstairs and take the picture off the wall. It was one of her better efforts, showing clearly the determined outline of her father's features. It had also been painted with love, and it showed. She only hoped André wouldn't comment on that.

He didn't, although she was sure he noticed it. 'Very good,' he approved. 'You really do have talent. Perhaps I will buy the one of me after all. I can keep it for my ancestors, if I ever have any.'

'Oh, you'll have some, I'm sure of it. And I'll give you the painting, but it probably won't be finished for months ahead. I'm very slow and meticulous. And I'll need plenty of sketches. I want to get your features from different angles and moods before I decide how I want to paint you.'

'When do you want to start?'

'How about right now?' Now that she had made the decision she didn't want to waste any time. She couldn't be sure of how long he was staying.

'Down here, or do you need to go up to your studio?'

'Here will be fine, although I'll just take this back upstairs and get my sketch pad. I'll have to rely on memory for skin tones and the colour of your eyes,' she muttered thoughtfully to herself as she left the room.

'I didn't know you'd looked at my eyes long enough to know what colour they are,' he commented when she returned to the lounge. 'I suppose we could always do a bit of gazing into each other's eyes. Yours are blue, I know that, but they could use a little more studying.'

'That won't be necessary,' she said primly. 'I know exactly what colour eyes you have.'

'Oh, what a shame!' André stood up and began unbuttoning his shirt.

As he began to slip it off his shoulders Caroline became rather worried. 'What are you doing?' she asked desperately.

'Taking off my clothes,' he said casually. 'I fancied a nude painting. You know, lounging on the sofa and all that.'

Caroline blushed a fiery red. 'I'm not painting you nude! I—I've never seen a man naked.'

He stopped in the process of undoing the button at the top of his trousers. 'Never?'

'Never,' she shook her head firmly.

He grinned broadly and pulled his shirt back on. 'If you could see your face, Caro!' he laughed openly now. 'I think I forgot to mention that I have a warped sense of humour. I had no intention of removing all my clothes, not for a painting anyway. God, your face was so funny!'

'Well, thank you! I'm glad I can provide you with a little light entertainment!' Caroline slammed the door behind her and ran up to her room.

CHAPTER SIX

ANDRÉ knocked on the door for the second time. 'Oh, come on, Caro. It was only a little harmless fun. You're so easy to tease, I couldn't resist it.'

His voice sounded clearly through the closed door, but Caroline pointedly ignored him. How dared he make fun of her like that! Warped sense of humour indeed—warped mind, more like!

'Don't be childish, Caro. I warned you I'd get you back for sinking your teeth into my hand. We're quits now. Don't be such a bad sport.'

She could feel herself weakening under his cajoling. She *had* bitten his hand, and he had warned her he would pay her back for it. At least he hadn't done her any physical damage as she had him, only embarrassed her a little. No, be honest, he had embarrassed her a lot. Her eyes had been drawn compulsively to his tanned body as he removed his shirt, and she had to admit it was a very attractive body. Wide powerful shoulders tapered down to a narrow waist, dark hair ran down his chest to his navel, and his skin was a deep mahogany brown, evidence of his time recently spent in the sun.

'Caro?' he persisted.

'All right.' She opened the door. 'And will you stop calling me by that name!'

'Don't you like it?' She could tell by the laughter still evident in his eyes that he was still amused by her embarrassment.

'It isn't that. It sounds—it gives people the wrong impression about us.'

'Brian Wells, you mean,' he guessed shrewdly. 'I'll

call you what I damn well please. Caro suits you better than Caroline.'

'All right. I've realised by now that you'll only do what you want to,' she sighed. 'You're so stubborn!'

'So are you. That's probably why we argue.' He took her arm. 'I'm ready for those sketches now. And no teasing this time.'

She looked up at him, seeing the difficulty he had controlling his mirth. She had to laugh, and he soon joined in. 'How far would you have gone if I hadn't stopped you?' she asked between chuckles.

'I'm not sure,' he answered truthfully. 'I can't really answer that—you did stop me, so my answer would be irrelevant. But I'm not ashamed of showing my body.'

She wasn't surprised. It was a firm muscled body, and he obviously kept himself in good physical condition, with none of the boardroom fat that seemed to trouble her father. This man looked after his body.

He sat down in the chair. 'So how do you want me?'

She raised a mocking eyebrow but forbore from making any comment. 'Just act normally, I don't want set poses.' She began to sketch in earnest, strong firm lines on the paper that soon began to take on the shape of André Gregory's face.

'Do you want to listen to some music?'

She shrugged, concentrating hard, her tongue resting on her bottom lip. 'I don't mind. If you feel you can relax better, go ahead.'

André stood up. 'I'm not tense. I just thought it might be nice to listen to some soft romantic music.'

Her look sharpened at his use of the word romantic, but he was no longer looking at her but at the varied record collection in the cabinet. The sure strong sound of Johnny Mathis soon pervaded the room, an old favourite with Caroline, and she smiled her pleasure. It was the perfect music for a relaxing evening, the sort of music for lovers to listen to. But they weren't lovers! Nor ever likely to be, no matter what her father said.

Several sketches later she sat back with a sigh. 'I think that's enough for today. I'll do some more to-morrow when I'm feeling fresher. Want to see?' She held up the four sketches she had done.

'Sure,' He came to stand next to her, leafing through them. There was one of him laughing, one simply smil-ing, another of him brooding and thoughtful, and finally one of him blazingly angry. He laughed when he came to this one. 'Do I really look like that?'

'When you're angry, yes. Very forbidding.'

'Mm.' He studied it a few moments longer, sitting on the arm of her chair, his arm resting across her shoulders. 'No wonder some of my business rivals look a bit subdued when they come up against me! I never realised I had that effect on people.'

She was very conscious of his hand on her shoulder, of its warmth against her skin. 'Believe me, I know. I've been on the receiving end.'

'Hm,' That hand began to massage her nape. 'Would you like me to make recompense for my bad humour of yesterday?' he asked softly, and looked down at her bent head.

'Feeling guilty?' Caroline cursed herself for the break in her voice. If only he would remove his hand, stop doing strange things to her senses!

'No, but I might enjoy making amends.' His voice was curiously close to her ear, and she squirmed be-neath his questing lips on her nape.

'Stop it, André,' she begged, trying to move away but finding it impossible in the confines of the chair.

'You should have said that the other evening,' he murmured. '*Then* I might have taken some notice of you. Right now I'm taking notice of nothing but my own senses. And they're telling me to go right on kissing you.'

'*Please*, André. Don't!' But she didn't really want him to stop. She loved the feel of his lips against her skin, not soft and moist like some men's but firm and sure and completely knowledgeable of her most sensitive areas, like the nape of her neck and the area of skin just below her ear. 'Stop it!' she pleaded.

'In a moment.' He spoke from deep within his throat, sliding off the arm of the chair and into the chair itself, their bodies pressed intimately together from shoulder to thigh. 'Did Wells kiss you like this?' he parted her lips probingly. 'Or like this?' now down to the hollow between her breasts. 'Or like this?' he undid the buttons of her blouse to further explore those rosy peaks that could be seen through the semi-transparency of the material.

'No,' she admitted in a strangulated voice. 'No one has ever kissed me like this before.'

'No one?' His mouth returned to tantalise hers, taking her lips and releasing them until she arched up against him in frustration, her mouth parted invitingly.

'No one,' she answered impatiently, not wanting to talk.

'Do you like it?' He was pressing slow languorous kisses against her creamy throat.

'I like it.' Her eyes were pleading, looking at that strong mouth only inches away from her own, so near and yet deliberately denied her. She knew André was well aware of his effect on her, that he revelled in her weakness almost. But it was a weakness she couldn't help, one that she couldn't deny, this longing for his caresses. Once again their verbal fencing had brought them to this weakening onslaught, and once again she couldn't deny him.

She moved against him now, making only moans of pleasure at his mouth on her own. His body lay across

hers, but it wasn't uncomfortable, more seduc...
he pressed her back against the chair until she c...
move no further, their bodies curved perfectly o...
against the other.

André slipped her blouse off one shoulder, his lips
travelling over the soft skin there with a sureness she
revelled in. 'This could become habit-forming,' he
murmured softly.

'What could?' She scarcely dared breathe lest she
break his mood.

He moved his head back slightly to look at her,
the dark swathe of hair across his forehead giving him
a rakish appearance. 'This could. This thing between
us that makes me want to either beat you or make love
to you. And I'm not sure which emotion is going to
win.'

Caroline breathed huskily. 'Which do you want to
win?' she whispered.

He gave a wry grin. 'Which do you think?'

'I—I'm not sure.' She avoided his eyes.

He gave a throaty laugh and bit her earlobe playfully. 'Right now, as close as we are, I'm sure you're
very much aware of what I want to do to you. But
I didn't come here with a casual love affair in mind,' he
added. 'So I think one of us will have to leave here
soon, before this situation gets out of control.'

The passion left her eyes and the reality of just
what she was inviting washed over her. She stiffened
in his arms. 'Do you ever *let* a situation get out of
control?' she taunted.

'If I want it to.'

'Do you never let anything happen spontane-
ously?'

André moved up and away from her, moving to look
down at the fire, his back towards her. 'I'm a man,
Caroline, not a boy. I've learnt to control my emotions
to a certain degree. Of course, there comes a time for

a man when it's too late to turn back, but I've never let things go that far if I don't know exactly what I'm doing.'

So it was back to Caroline now! 'But you—you must have made love—— You have a lot of experience!' That much was obvious!

'I admit that, but on those occasions I've known exactly what was going to happen from the beginning of our evening together.'

'You—you make it all sound so—so clinical!'

'Oh, no,' he turned to look at her. 'It's enjoyable, very enjoyable. But if a woman shows me she doesn't want that sort of relationship it doesn't make me determined to win her over. I've never wanted a woman that badly.'

Her eyes widened indignantly. 'But I—I'm sure I never——'

'No, you didn't,' he frowned. 'But I do want you, that's why I'm saying one of us will have to leave.'

'Well, it isn't going to be me. You're being silly about this, allowing two random incidents to colour your judgment.'

'Random?' He shook his head. 'They aren't random at all. I feel like this most of the time, and you don't help the situation, flaunting yourself and arguing with me most of the time.'

'I didn't deliberately seek you out this afternoon, *you* did that.'

'That was because this cottage isn't big enough for you to carry out the frosty not-speaking act. That fishing expedition was a way for you to get over your sulks and still save face.'

'Well, thanks! I don't need——'

André sighed. 'Caroline! Will you calm down? I'm not sure I can cope with this love-hate relationship. Just try to dampen down this emotionalism a little, hmm?'

'Go to hell!'

'More coffee, André?' Eve Gresham smiled at him enquiringly.

'Thank you,' he nodded acceptance.

The four of them were sitting in the lounge of the farmhouse, the debris from their meal all cleared away by the two women. Dinner had been enjoyable—melon, coq-au-vin accompanied by baby potatoes, peas and carrots, followed by cheese and biscuits, and finished by the creamy coffee they were now sipping.

They had dropped the formality of Mr Gregory and Miss Rawlings after the first few minutes of conversation, for which Caroline felt relieved, having forgotten who 'Miss Rawlings' was a couple of times. She and André were barely speaking to each other; after last night's little episode she thought the least contact they had the better.

She might be going to turn the tables on him in the end, but at the moment each time he took her in his arms the situation got out of control—for her at least, and she felt sure André had no more control over the happenings at the time than she did.

He sat on the sofa next to Eve Gresham, dressed more formally than usual in black trousers and black roll-necked jumper, and a cream jacket. The whole effect was devastating and Caroline had felt her senses heighten just at the sight of him. They had driven over together in his car, and his close proximity had only made her more aware of his warm vital body only inches from her own.

'Caroline?'

She looked up to see Eve Gresham hovering over her with the coffee pot.

'Er—no—no, thank you.'

Eve smiled. 'You seem far away.'

Caroline returned the smile, liking this woman even

while resenting her attitude towards André. That Eve found him attractive was undeniable and Caroline watched his every move for a sign that the feeling was reciprocated. André gave no indication of such feelings, treating all three of his dining companions with the same polite courtesy—perhaps a little coolly towards Caroline, but that was only to be expected.

'I was thinking of André's attempt at fishing,' she remarked, giving him a sly look.

Brian looked at the other man. 'Did you go today?'

'Yesterday, for a short time,' André remarked calmly. 'My first attempt, it won't be repeated.'

'It's an acquired taste,' laughed Eve. 'Brian isn't too keen either, but our father loved it.'

'Would you like to see the kitten while you're here?' Brian asked her softly, but his sister heard him.

'It's cold and dark out there, Brian,' she scolded.

'Not in the barn it isn't,' he grinned. 'Debbie wouldn't allow her precious cats to be cold. I've had to put a storage heater out there for their comfort,' he told them.

'But it's cold outside,' his sister insisted. 'It's quite a distance to the barn. Why not come over tomorrow and see them instead?'

'That appears to be a better idea,' put in André. 'I have to be leaving in a few minutes, and Caroline will be going with me.'

Eve's face showed her disappointment. 'But it's early yet. Stay a while longer,' she pressed.

He shook his head. 'Impossible, I'm afraid. Dinner has been lovely, but I'm expecting an important call at ten-thirty.'

Caroline looked up in surprise. As far as she was aware André had had contact with no one since his arrival at the cottage—except for her father, and she felt sure it wasn't a call from him. She wondered who the important call could be from. Probably one of his women. And this didn't please her either.

'I can take you home later if you want, Caroline,' Brian suggested eagerly. 'Eve's right, it's early yet.'

She was curious about André's call. 'I think I should leave with André,' she refused. 'I've really enjoyed this evening, thank you.'

André stood up. 'Are you ready to leave?' he asked abruptly. 'It's almost ten o'clock now and I don't want to miss that call.' He turned to their hostess. 'Thanks for the meal, Eve. I'm only sorry we have to leave so early.'

'That's all right,' she smiled brightly. 'You'll have to come again.'

'Oh, we will,' he agreed politely.

'You'll come down tomorrow?' Brian asked Caroline privately. 'To see Bobby,' he added persuasively.

'All right,' she accepted. 'In the afternoon some time.'

The silence in the car was becoming oppressive. 'You were a bit abrupt weren't you?' Her voice sounded very loud against the previous silence.

'No one forced you to leave,' he replied tautly. 'Wells would have been only too pleased to have brought you home later—with a prolonged goodnight, I have no doubt.'

'You sound almost jealous,' she returned lightly.

'Don't be so damned ridiculous!' he exploded, his face furious. Caroline visibly looked surprised by his reaction to her teasing comment. 'I'm merely looking after Matt's interests for him,' he added.

'I'm sure he would appreciate it—although he doesn't expect it,' she threw back at him.

'Just what does he expect?' he asked, dangerously soft. 'I know Matt of old—he's devious, shrewd, and not above manipulating people to get his own way. So why has he left the two of us together at his cottage? Why doesn't he demand that one of us leave? I know damn well I wouldn't let you live like this if you were mine!'

'He did demand that one of us leave—me,' she told him hotly. 'And I refused.'

'Because you were here first,' he taunted. 'That still doesn't explain why he hasn't driven up here and forcibly dragged you away.'

She smiled, trying to visualise her father acting so physically—and failing miserably. 'That isn't his way and you know it. At least, you should do, if you know him at all well.'

'Oh, I know him,' André said grimly. 'And there are a few things about this set-up that I'm not too sure about, a few pertinent questions Matt could give me answers to if he cared to—which I'm sure he doesn't.'

'All this doesn't explain why you were so rude to Eve Gresham and her brother.'

'I wasn't rude, merely a little terse. I don't like getting involved in the domestic scene, with talk of children and animals. I could almost feel the matrimonial noose tightening around my neck.'

'Now who's being ridiculous? They were merely a nice couple trying to make us welcome. Eve may have been a little——' she hesitated, 'well a little ...'

'Over enthusiastic in her attentions, is what I think you're trying to say,' he finished dryly.

'Well ... maybe a little,' she admitted.

'I would say a lot. She's a very beautiful and attractive woman, she shouldn't try to sell herself short.' He parked the car. 'There must be plenty of men who would appreciate her as a wife, and think themselves lucky for gaining such a prize.'

'But not you,' Caroline stated. They were in the cottage now and she reached instinctively for the kettle, intending to make a warming drink.

'Leave it,' he ordered. 'I feel like a whisky.' He strode into the lounge, pouring himself a large amount of the fiery liquid and drinking some quickly before pouring some out for her.

She watched him drink the rest of the liquid without a wince, sipping tentatively at her own. Goodness, he was angry! She avoided looking at the stormy green eyes, although she could see the tension start to leave his body as the liquid began to soothe his frayed nerves.

'Not me,' he finally agreed, slamming down his empty glass. 'That sort of thing doesn't interest me.'

Caroline frowned. 'What sort of thing?'

'Eve Gresham makes no secret of the fact that she's on the lookout for a husband, someone who'll take her away from this life.' He took off his cream jacket and threw it over a chair. 'I don't get involved with those sort of ladies.'

'Oh no,' she smiled bitterly. 'You only like the ones that know the score.'

'It isn't that, Caro,' he muttered, running a hand through the thickness of his hair. 'Surely you could see what was happening? If I hadn't stepped in, for all her protestations to the contrary, Eve would have finally agreed that it was a good idea for you to go and see the kittens. She didn't want to appear too eager, but she would have agreed to the suggestion eventually. And that would have left me alone with her.'

'And you didn't want that.' Her heart was still beating at a fast rate from his renewed use of the shortened version of her first name. She noticed that every time he was angry with her he resorted to the more formal Caroline, so perhaps their disagreement was at an end.

'No, I didn't. Can you blame me?'

'It's nothing to do with me.'

'It has everything to do with you!' He moved closer to her, the long length of his thigh almost touching her own. 'I'm living here in close proximity with you. You're attractive, very attractive—no, damn it, you're beautiful. And you attract me, but you already know that. And while we're living together like this I can't think of anyone else but you.' He smiled as her eyes widened. 'The spontaneous feelings you seem to think I never have—well, they're all there. And I don't like it.'

Caroline turned away. 'But you said——'

'Yes, I did,' he interrupted. 'But I also said with you I thought things might get out of hand. Well, I think they're just about to ...'

He pulled her against him, bending his dark head to claim her lips with savage intensity. She was crushed hard against him, her hands resting on his chest, caught between the two of them. He was holding her so tightly she felt as if she were going to snap in half at any moment.

But she soon forgot everything but the feel of those lips and the way his hands held her immovable against his hard unyielding flesh. Her lips returned the pressure of his and she revelled in his power over her. Why deny it any longer, she was fast falling in love with this attractive stranger, was even now so much in love with him she couldn't think straight. She acknowledged it even while wanting to deny it. Her mind fought against him and his closeness even while her body melted against him.

'Oh, Caro,' he groaned against her lips. 'Why do you affect me like this?' He teased and played with her lips for long agonising seconds before increasing their pressure once again, their mutual passion rising to fever pitch. 'You wore this dress on purpose,' he muttered. 'You must know how good you look in it.'

It was a black silk dress and clung in all the right places, and she did know it suited her. Why not— clothes were meant to suit their wearer. 'I didn't wear it on purpose,' she denied, loving the feel of his lips against her throat.

'Perhaps not, you look good in anything. Staying here together like this is explosive.' He had slowly undone the zip of her dress several inches to gently caress her shoulders. 'Are you willing to take the consequences?'

'Consequences?' Caroline was lost in the vortex of her own feelings, her senses aflame with desire.

'In a few minutes I'm going to carry you up those stairs to my bedroom, close the door, throw you on the bed, and not let you out until tomorrow if I let you out then.'

She licked her suddenly dry lips. 'I——'

'It's no good arguing, Caro,' his voice was husky. 'I warned you yesterday, gave you every chance to get out, now it's too late. I think I've already reached the point of no return where you're concerned. In fact, I'm way past.'

As she had never been made love to fully before the thought of it terrified her—excited, but terrified her too. 'But—but Matt! He——'

Already André was turning towards the door, her hand held firmly in his own. 'If it only happens the once then it's up to you whether you tell him or not, and if we get a relationship of our own going then I'll explain to him how it is between us,' he told her calmly.

She could just imagine her father's reaction to that! 'No, I—I don't think I——' She was interrupted by the ringing of the telephone.

André held her back from answering it. 'Leave it, Caro. I want you, *now*.'

She pulled away from him. 'It could be that call you're expecting.'

'I'm not expecting a call, that was just a way of being able to leave without seeming too rude.'

'But I—I have to answer it.' She picked up the receiver. 'Caroline R—Rawlings speaking.'

'Do I have the Rayner cottage?' It was a female voice, low and what Caroline would guess most men would call sexy. She felt her hackles rise, as she held out the receiver to André. 'I think it's for you,' she said resentfully. No telephone call indeed!

He snatched the receiver out of her hand. 'Gregory here,' he said curtly. 'Oh, hello, Sylvia. No, I hadn't forgotten you were going to call me. Who answered the telephone?' He glanced at Caroline's set face. 'That was the girl I'm sharing the cottage with. No, it isn't like that,' he gave a throaty chuckle. 'No, no. Why do you always think the worst?'

Caroline was in the process of opening the lounge door to leave when his voice stopped her. She turned to face him at the sound of her name. 'Yes?' she asked sharply.

He had his hand over the mouthpiece. 'Where are you going?' Passion still burnt for her in his eyes.

'To my room. To bed. Alone. To sleep.'

'I'll be finished here in a moment. If you'll just wait——'

'You have a nerve!' she burst out angrily. 'Just finish talking to your girl-friend and don't give me another thought. I won't be giving you any.'

'Caro!' he sighed in exasperation.

She didn't bother to answer him, but left the room. The damned nerve of the man! She hadn't intended going to bed with him anyway, but for him to think he could just carry on where he left off after speaking to one of his girl-friends was just downright arrogance on his part. But then he was arrogant, to the point of being insufferable.

She had been in bed a full five minutes when she heard him making his way up the stairs. Without any preliminary warning he walked into her bedroom, not at all concerned with the look of outraged indignation on her face. She put down the book she had been pretending an interest in, pulling herself into a sitting position.

'What do you think you're doing in here?' She sounded angry enough, but inside she was quaking. What if he decided he was going to take her with or without her permission?

He looked around him interestedly, finally bringing those hard green eyes to rest on her, pinning her slender body to the bed with their rapier sharpness. 'What do you think I'm here for?' he asked softly.

She plumped up the pillows energetically. 'I told you, no. Especially after ...'

'After a harmless conversation with my secretary. Oh yes,' he insisted. 'Sylvia is my secretary, and a very competent one too. I admit I was expecting her to call me some time while I was here, but certainly not this evening. Apparently she'd been calling me all day.'

'Does it matter why she called? It happened. It's over. The mood is broken now.'

André gave a mocking smile. 'You coward! Can't you admit that you had no intention of going to bed with me, admit you would have got out of it any way you could. You're what's commonly known as a tease, a damned little tease!'

'I'm not! I never said I would go to bed with you, not once did I say such a thing.'

'You didn't need to. You weren't exactly fighting me all the way, were you? No wonder Matt didn't make sure you left here, he knew I wouldn't get anywhere with you. You tempt a man, drive him almost insane with wanting you, and then you freeze.' His face was full of cold contempt for her. 'There's nothing there, is there, Caroline? You have all the beauty and the body of a temptress, and yet when it comes down to it you're cold, you have nothing to give a man at all!'

Caroline had sat almost open-mouthed during this

tirade. 'Is that the way you usually explain away your inadequacies? Blame the woman?'

'Don't try turning the tables on me,' he said patiently. 'I'm not falling for that one. You were terrified when I said I was taking you to my room.'

'I—I wasn't,' she denied, fidgeting unnecessarily with the coverlet on her bed. 'You—you were rushing things, going too fast for me. A few kisses don't necessarily mean I have to jump into bed with you.'

'They weren't just kisses and you know it!'

'Don't overestimate yourself, André. Like I said, a few kisses don't mean I have to start a full-scale affair with you.' Again she tried to sound self-confident, but wasn't sure if she had succeeded, for André's face gave little away.

'That's true. In that case these incidents will have to stop. I'm no boy and I can't be satisfied with the little you're prepared to give.'

'So now we understand each other.' She swallowed hard. 'I'll stay out of your way if you'll stay out of mine.'

He smiled distantly. 'We said that in the beginning, but it doesn't seem to have worked.'

'No,' she admitted. 'All right, you win.' She came to a decision, realising that in the light of her discovered love for this man she couldn't handle this situation any longer, if she ever could, which she doubted. 'I'll leave. Give me a day or so to get myself together and I'll get out of your hair.'

'Great.' He closed the door softly behind him.

'Bobby looks happier now he's back with his brothers and sisters,' Caroline remarked, smiling up at Brian before looking back at the young kittens falling playfully over their mother.

'I'm glad you came back today.'

'I came to say goodbye,' she said regretfully. 'I'm

leaving today or tomorrow.' She would be genuinely sorry to say goodbye to Brian, she had enjoyed her times with him.

Brian caught her by the shoulders. 'But why are you leaving? I thought you were here on holiday.'

'Not really.' She pushed back her long swathe of hair. 'I was just staying at the cottage for a few days. I—it's—well, it isn't working out, André and I sharing. We—we don't get on.'

'I see.' He pursed his lips thoughtfully, opening the farmhouse door for her to enter the kitchen. I thought there was a little friction between you yesterday evening.'

'Not a little—a lot. No matter how much I would like to do so André isn't the sort of person I can ignore.' Far from it! He didn't just annoy her now, he was becoming part of her life, a part she didn't want to give up. But she would! Once in London she would push him out of her life, pick up with the old crowd and carry on where she had left off. Well, she would give it a good try anyway.

'But do you have to leave? You could—you could stay here with us,' Brian suggested eagerly. 'Eve would be glad of the company, and I—well, I——'

She touched his hand gently. 'Thanks, Brian, but no, thanks. I have to get back to London, I have people to see.' Her father for one!

'But you'll come back?'

'I don't know, I doubt it.'

She drove slowly back to the cottage, her thoughts solely on André Gregory. Somehow he had found his way into her heart, and she couldn't understand how it had happened. They were either arguing violently or in each other's arms, and surely that was no basis for love? And yet she had never felt this way about any man before, as if nothing they ever did together could be wrong in her eyes.

She might have felt nervous of these feelings the night before, but she also knew that if André took her in his arms again she would react the same way. She was like butter in his hands, her head a mindless void, and her will-power nil.

At least since her decision to leave he had been polite—very curt, but polite. Caroline had hoped that by today he might have changed his mind about wanting her to go, but his attitude gave no such indication. In fact the air had been so tense between them this morning that she had decided to visit Brian after lunch.

The cold air hit her again as she got out of the car and she quickly locked up and let herself into the cottage. All was quiet inside, although she thought she heard a faint rustle of paper in the lounge. André was probably in there; should she go in and disturb him or not? Oh hell, why not! She was leaving soon anyway.

He was seated at the table, papers strewn out before him. 'You're working?' she asked politely.

His look was scornful. 'It would appear so.'

She made an effort not to be angry. 'I thought you were here to rest.'

'I am, but this work couldn't wait, hence Sylvia's phone call last night.' He sat back. 'I've finished now.' He began to collect up the papers.

'You don't have to clear away because of me,' she told him airily. 'I promise not to sneak a look at any of your papers.'

'You wouldn't find out anything even if you did. And I was packing up anyway. I have to get these things off to my secretary today.'

'I—I've been over to see Brian this afternoon.'

'Oh yes?'

'Mmm, I went to say goodbye.'

He appeared preoccupied with his papers. 'You already told me you were leaving.'

'So I did.' She was hurt by his casual attitude, but made an effort not to show it.

André picked up his attaché case and began to put away his papers. 'So obviously you would want to see Wells before you leave.'

Caroline watched his unhurried movements, noting vaguely the gold initials on the side of his attaché case. A.G.F. She looked again, it definitely said A.G.F.' she wasn't mistaken. She licked her lips. 'Your case,' she indicated it.

'Mm?' At last he looked up.

'The initials on the attaché case, they aren't yours,' she stated.

André looked down at the lid. 'They aren't?'

'No,' she shook her head.

'But they are.'

'They can't be, your name is André Gregory. How can they be A.G.F.?'

'Quite easily. André Gregory isn't my full name.'

'It isn't?' she had a terrible feeling of foreboding, as if she wasn't going to like his answer to her next question. 'What is your full name?'

'André Gregory Fortnum,' he stated calmly.

CHAPTER SEVEN

'GREG FORTNUM!' The name came out in a gasp.

He carried on tidying away his papers, not realising the bombshell he had dropped in her little world. 'Does it matter?' He shut the case with a snap, coming over to sit in the chair facing her own.

Did it matter! Caroline had gone first cold and now hot, sick and now strangely empty. This man was Greg Fortnum, the man her father had suggested she marry, the man she had come here to get away from. She felt slightly hysterical. For five days she had been sharing a cottage with the dreaded Greg Fortnum! And her father had known that! She looked sharply at the man opposite her; had he known all the time that he was living with Caroline *Rayner*? The completely relaxed look on his face said no.

'Caroline?' he probed gently. 'Does it matter?' he repeated.

'Of course it matters! You've been deceiving me. Greg Fortnum indeed! And—and Matt kept quiet about it too.' This was what angered her the most, her father's deception. He had known all along that she was staying here with this man, and he had done nothing to warn her. If she found out this man had been deceiving her on purpose too ...

He shrugged. 'I asked him to. I came here to relax, and I never seem to be able to do that as Greg Fortnum, so I just omitted the last part of my name. It worked.'

'Yes, it did,' she said crossly. 'You had no right to do it.'

'Why? It didn't hurt anyone, and it gave me the

privacy I badly needed.' He gave a rueful grin. 'And my plea of needing complete rest got me out of meeting Matt's daughter—I'd do anything to get out of that.'

So he had answered her question for her. He still didn't know who she was. Now that she knew he was Greg Fortnum it didn't seem very important to her either. Her father had played a dirty trick on both of them, and when she got back to London ... 'You really don't like her, do you?'

'I don't like what I've heard of her,' he corrected. 'Never having met the young lady myself I can hardly give an accurate opinion, but I would say she's a thoroughly spoilt little girl who ought to be brought down a peg or two.'

'And you're just the man to do it?' she suggested sarcastically. Really, just where did he get his information!

'I could be,' he agreed. 'In the right circumstances.'

'I can imagine what they might be!'

'Mmm. Well, now you know who I really am, does it make you feel any differently towards me?'

'Oh yes, it makes it all the easier to leave. You see, you have quite a reputation, and it isn't a good one. I'm not sure I would like it to become public knowledge that I've spent five days alone in a secluded cottage with the notorious womaniser Greg Fortnum.'

'What difference does my name make? It would still have been five days spent alone with a comparative stranger, no matter what my name is. It didn't seem to bother you before.'

'Of course it bothered me,' she said indignantly. 'I just didn't see why I should be forced to leave because of you. But you had to try and live up to your reputation, didn't you?' she added in a scoffing voice.

His eyes narrowed. 'What do you mean?'

She smiled. 'All those moves, the pretence that with

me it could have been different—it's all a line to you.
I bet you tell each new conquest the same rubbish.'

André looked bored. 'I don't usually need to.'

'I can imagine. Only this time it didn't work. I
didn't like you before, André—Greg—oh, damn! But
I like you even less now. Greg Fortnum!' she finished
in disgust.

'André will do, it does happen to be my true name.'

'Then why bother with Greg?' she snapped.

He shrugged. 'It seems to be the name my business
associates prefer, not so flowery as André, I should
imagine. A few very close friends, and my family still
call me André.'

'Well, I don't fit into either category, and have no
wish to, so from now on I'll call you Greg.' Caroline
turned her head away.

'You won't have much opportunity to call me anything. You're leaving, remember?'

'Oh—oh, yes.'

'You hadn't forgotten?'

Her eyes flashed. 'Only momentarily. It isn't every
day you find out that the famous Greg Fortnum has
been making passes at you—it came as quite a shock.
I wouldn't have expected someone like you to take
a holiday here, I would have thought somewhere like
the Bahamas was more to your taste than a tiny cottage
in Cumbria.'

'No privacy. When Matt suggested this cottage it
seemed ideal. But every Eden has its serpent.'

'You're so rude!'

'I know,' he replied uncaringly.

Caroline stood up. 'I'm just going to pack my
things.'

'No one's attempting to stop you.'

After a momentary hesitation between slapping his
face and storming out of the room she decided on the
latter. It seemed the safest; he was probably the sort

of man who would hit her back.

Ten minutes later she was back downstairs, her packed suitcase in her hand. André—Greg was reading a book beside the fire. 'I'm off, then.'

He glanced up, turning over a page of his book. 'Have a safe journey,' he remarked before returning his attention to the book.

'Do you really care?' she snapped.

'Of course, I have the usual respect for human life.'

'But nothing else?' she probed.

André sighed, discarding the book completely. 'What else could there be? You want to leave, so I wish you a safe journey. What else can I say?'

'Nothing, apparently.' Caroline turned to the door, her hand already outstretched to turn the handle when she felt him close behind her.

'Caro?' He took hold of her shoulders and turned her round. 'Do you want to go?'

She shrugged. 'I have to.'

'You don't have to do anything you don't want to do. If you want to stay, stay, if you want to go, go. But don't expect me to beg you to stay, because I won't.'

'I didn't expect you to.'

He removed his hands and stepped back. 'So, make up your mind, either go or stay, but for goodness' sake make a decision one way or the other. You haven't been this unsure in your other decisions, you decided you didn't like me from the start, and I don't think I've done anything to change that.'

'No.' He hadn't done anything, but she had; she had fallen in love with him!

'Then you'd better go.'

Caroline went, revving up the car angrily before accelerating out of the driveway. How she managed to drive home she didn't know, only coming to an awareness of her surroundings as she stopped in the courtyard of their apartment block. She hadn't caused any accidents, so she couldn't have driven that badly.

It was pitch black now, although it was only six o'clock, still much too early for her father to be home. Perhaps that was just as well; she hadn't completely calmed down from his deception yet, and she didn't want to explode at him as soon as she entered the apartment.

She let herself in with her key, turning with a smile as Maggie came out to see who had entered. 'Only me, Maggie. The prodigal returns.'

'Caroline!' the elderly housekeeper greeted her with enthusiasm. 'Thank goodness you're back!'

'Daddy proving more unbearable than usual?' Caroline took a guess at Maggie's relief at seeing her. She usually managed to cushion things between the two of them, knowing that although her father had threatened hundreds of times to give Maggie her notice, he would never do it. They both loved her too much to do without her.

Maggie grinned, her face older now, but still as beautiful as Caroline remembered her as a child. To Caroline, Maggie had become the mother figure lacking in her life, and it was to her she had run when her first love affair had gone wrong at the great age of twelve, to her she had shown with pride her first evening gown, and to her she had proudly presented her first 'grown up' boy-friend. Yes, Maggie was an important part of the household, and although some people would say she was only an employee, to Caroline and her father she was much more.

'No more than usual,' Maggie retorted dryly. 'He's been a bit brash about your absence. He said you'd been to the cottage.'

Caroline walked into her bedroom, flinging her case on the bed to begin removing her neatly packed clothing. 'I have.'

Maggie shivered. 'A bit cold for that. What did you do for entertainment?'

She almost spluttered with laughter. Entertainment was something she hadn't gone short of. 'I met a couple from a neighbouring farm. The man took me out a couple of times.'

Maggie's eyebrows rose, and she took over Caroline's task with a frown. 'Didn't his wife object?'

'Oh, she wasn't his wife.' Caroline did laugh this time, Maggie's scandalised face was very amusing. And she needed amusement at the moment. 'Maggie, really! She was his sister.'

Her brow cleared. 'Oh—oh, I see. Only your father was muttering horrible threats about some man the other day, something to do with you, and I——'

'That would be Mr Fortnum, Maggie. You know Daddy's plans concerning him.'

'Hmp.' Maggie crossed her arms across her chest. 'Why doesn't he let you make your own mind up about the man you want to marry? I told him exactly what I thought of his latest idea.'

'You tell him altogether too much, Maggie,' Caroline grinned. 'That's why you argue.'

'We argue because he's a very stubborn man.'

'And you're a stubborn woman.' It felt good to be back among the normality of her family life, good to be away from Greg Fortnum.

'That's as maybe, but I'm sure he'll be glad to have you home again. And so am I. It's no fun cooking for one, especially someone as finicky as your father.'

Yes, it was definitely good to be back. Caroline grinned at Maggie. 'Don't count on me to cheer him up by appearing like this. He isn't going to like it at all.'

'He isn't?'

She gave a shake of her head. 'I'm sure of it.' She had thwarted his plans coming back like this, and he wouldn't forgive her easily.

Maggie shrugged. 'Well, you know best. But I would have thought he would be pleased to see you at any time.' She looked at her watch. 'He'll be home soon, I'll just go and put dinner on.'

'Nothing too much for me, Maggie. I'm not feeling too hungry.' And she wasn't, her appetite had deserted her since she had found out who André actually was. And she didn't think her father would be all that hungry when she had finished with him.

'You'll eat what I give you,' Maggie returned sternly. 'We don't have snack meals in any establishment I cook for.'

'Yes, Maggie.'

'And none of your cheek either. I may be pleased to see you home, but I won't have any of your non-sense.'

'No, Maggie.'

Maggie laughed at her mock-subdued look. 'You always could twist me round your little finger.'

'Yes, Maggie,' Caroline laughed too.

She was seated in the lounge when she heard her father enter the apartment, a glass of sherry in her hand, a soothing record playing on the stero unit.

'What the——?' Her father stopped in his tracks at the obvious habitation of the room, his eyes opening wide as she slowly stood up. 'Caroline!'

'The one and only,' she smiled tightly.

'But I——' he looked around. 'Are you here alone?'

'Who else would be with me?' she queried mildly, much more mildly than she felt.

'No one, I suppose. I just thought——' he shook his head.

'What did you think?'

He grimaced. 'You said you weren't coming home just yet. I'm naturally surprised to see you.'

'And pleased too?'

'What a damned stupid question to ask your own father!' He glared at her fiercely.

'But a pertinent one, wouldn't you say, considering you haven't even given me a hug hello, let alone a kiss,' she scoffed.

He came forward sheepishly to hug and kiss her. 'I am pleased to see you, love. But why didn't you let me know you were coming home today? I could have taken the afternoon off.'

Caroline moved away, a slight figure in a slim-fitting brown woollen dress. 'There was no need,' she told him distantly. 'And it was a spur-of-the-moment thing, not planned at all.

'I see.' He bit his bottom lip thoughtfully.

'Do you?' she said sharply.

Matt looked at her, shrewdly noting the high colour to her cheeks and the challenging sparkle to her eyes. 'Out with it, Caroline,' he sighed. 'I'm too old for these guessing games.'

She gave a mocking smile. 'Don't bring your age into this, you're fifty-two years of age, not a hundred. And you know damn well why I'm so angry.'

'Don't swear, Caroline. You know I don't like it.'

'Don't change the subject, Daddy,' she snapped at him. 'You're a deceitful, scheming, interfering old man, and I ought to hate you.'

'But you don't,' he stated with a smile. 'Now just tell me what I'm supposed to have done, and calmly, so that I can understand you.'

'You know very well what you've done. Greg Fortnum!'

'Greg?' He raised his eyebrows innocently. 'What about him?'

'Ooh, Daddy, I ought to hit you! You deliberately omitted to tell me I was staying at the cottage with him. André Gregory indeed! You knew how I felt about that man, you *knew*!'

'I know you didn't want me matchmaking, and I wasn't doing that. I wasn't within a hundred-mile radius, so how could I interfere?'

'Don't act the innocent with me! You could have told me who he was, stopped me making a fool of myself.'

'Did you do that?'

'You must know I did. I only found out this afternoon who he was.' And she could still remember her shock, too vividly for comfort.

'And that made you leave so suddenly,' he probed, watching her closely.

Caroline turned away. 'No, I'd already decided to leave before that. Finding out he was Greg Fortnum only made me all the more eager to go.'

'So you didn't like him?'

'No, I didn't!' she denied vehemently, perhaps too vehemently. 'He was everything I thought he would be, bossy, overbearing, sure of his own attraction—too damned sure of that.' She saw him frown. 'Damn isn't exactly swearing, Daddy.'

'It is to me,' he rebuked sternly.

'All right, all right!' she said impatiently. 'But you could have told me, you didn't have to let me find out like that.'

'Like what?'

She avoided his eyes. 'Like I did.'

'Mm, I see. Well, I didn't tell you because Greg asked me not to.'

'That was because he considered me to be your mistress,' she sighed her frustration. 'But you could have told me, your own daughter!'

'I could have,' he admitted. 'But I didn't see why I should. You left here in a fit of temper, leaving me to cope with our weekend guest on my own. I didn't see why I should make your stay at the cottage a pleasant one.'

'It wasn't!'

He chuckled. 'I can see that. But it wouldn't have made any difference to you if you'd know André was Greg Fortnum, he's still the same man, no matter what his name is.'

'It would have made a great deal of difference,' she told him crossly. 'I would have left at the first opportunity.'

'Perhaps that's why I kept quiet. You had a lesson in manners coming to you, Caroline, and Greg was just the man to give you it. By your attitude towards him I would say he succeeded.'

'He did not! He couldn't teach anyone manners, because he doesn't have any himself. He was rude to me from the first moment we met. I told you I was going to try and teach him a lesson—did that sound as if he had made a good impression?'

'He never tries to make a good impression. You take him as you find him, if you don't like what you find then that's too bad.'

'I didn't!'

'If you protest much more, Caroline, I'll begin to think you really liked him.'

'Then you would be wrong.' She didn't like the man, she *loved* him. 'Now don't try and wheedle out of the blame, Daddy. You kept quiet about his identity for reasons of your own, not because he asked you to. You wanted me to fall in love with him, wanted me to marry him. Well, I didn't, and I'm not going to. And did it ever occur to you to ask *him* if he wanted to get married?' She paced the room restlessly. 'He has no more desire to get married than I have.'

'I thought you would change all that.'

'I didn't. I wouldn't even attempt to try.'

'That's that then. Over. Finished. Now can we get on with the rest of our lives?'

Caroline wished she could dismiss it as easily as

he appeared to be able to. But she couldn't; she couldn't dismiss André at all. She found that she could never think of him as Greg for a start, to her he would always be André.

But she tried to forget him, she tried very hard over the next few days, going to a couple of parties and losing herself in shopping sprees during the daytime. By the fourth day of her return she had had enough, wanting only to go back to the cottage to see André. The carefully applied rosy hue couldn't hide the paleness of her cheeks, or disguise the dullness of her eyes.

'You look as if you could do with a holiday,' remarked Esther, as the two of them sat in Esther's compact but easy to run flat.

Caroline sipped her black coffee. 'I've only just had one.'

'It doesn't look as if it's done you much good. You look thoroughly fed up. Why don't you ask your father to let you go to your villa in the Bahamas? You need the sunshine.'

'I need André!' Caroline cried, her coffee cup landing with a clatter in the saucer.

'André?' Esther prompted. Caroline had been very reluctant to talk about her stay at the cottage, but she knew something was troubling her friend badly.

'André Gregory *Fortnum*!' Caroline said resentfully, her anger still not diminished by the passing of time.

'*André* Fortnum?' Esther queried softly.

'That's right. That's his full name.'

'And?'

'And I've been staying at the cottage with him,' she burst out fiercely.

'Oh.'

'And it was all Daddy's fault,' she carried on angrily. 'He ordered me back home knowing full well I would do the opposite, all the time knowing I was staying there with that hateful Greg Fortnum. I'll never forgive him. Never!'

'Explain from the beginning, Caroline,' Esther interrupted gently. 'You aren't making a lot of sense at the moment.'

She listened patiently to Caroline's often not very articulate explanation, her eyebrows raised in surprise at the end of the tirade. 'So all the time you were staying with Greg Fortnum?'

'Don't call him that!' she literally winced with the pain it caused her. 'His name is André.'

'So how do you feel about him now?' Esther tried not to look too interested in the answer.

'How can I feel about him?' Caroline cried. 'You know my opinion of Greg Fortnum, why I didn't even want to meet him. He's a rake, Esther, an out-and-out rake!'

'And André?'

'André——?' Caroline looked startled, then shrugged resignedly. 'They're the same person.'

'Not to you they aren't,' Esther smiled. 'Look at this thing reasonably, Caroline. I realise that it's difficult at the moment, but just try. If you hadn't heard of his reputation via other people, what would you have thought of him? What do you know of him that you haven't heard through the media or other similar sources?'

'Why, nothing——'

'There you are, then,' said Esther with satisfaction.

'But Daddy says he's very ruthless.'

'Of course he is, most good businessmen are. Your father's the same, but that doesn't stop you loving him.'

'I don't love Andr—Greg Fortnum!'

'I agree with you about the latter, but André ...'

Esther shook her head. 'You feel quite differently about him.'

Caroline's shoulders slumped as she admitted defeat. 'You're right, I love—*like* him a lot. He's so different from anyone else I've ever met. But we argued nearly all the time I was there, and not very pleasant arguments at that.'

'That's to be expected, you're both strong personalities.'

Caroline gave a rueful grin. 'André's that all right. But he's very attractive,' she added.

'Mm, I've seen photographs of him.'

Caroline grimaced. 'I wish I had, I could have saved myself all this heartache and left at the first sight of him. And to think I stayed on to teach the arrogant devil a lesson! I don't know where he got his information about me from, but he has the most terrible opinion of my morals. And he was very rude about Daddy's matchingmaking plans.'

'Well, so were you, so you have something in common. And at a guess I would say he got his information the same place you got yours. That just proves how wrong they can be. His opinion of you was the reason for your change of surname?'

'Yes,' Caroline nibbled disinterestedly at a biscuit. 'I never did tell him who I really am, it didn't seem important under the circumstances.'

Esther shook her head. 'I would have said it was very important. Oh, Caroline,' she scolded, 'can't you see that the affair he thought you were having with Matt was the main reason he half despised you?'

'*Half* despised!'

Esther chuckled. 'It didn't sound to me as if that was all he felt towards you.'

Caroline remembered her candid disclosures of a few minutes earlier and blushed profusely. 'No—no, I suppose not. But it wouldn't have worked, Esther.

You know my feeling regarding love and marriage. I won't compromise by having an affair with anyone, no matter how they attract me. I want a normal happy marriage, like yours. You know that's why I've never entered into any of the casual relationships most of the crowd find *amusing*. They just don't interest me.'

'Are you sure an affair was all he was interested in? He seemed to find you—irresistible.'

'It was a mutual attraction. But he more or less told me that if a girl isn't willing to give her all, he isn't interested.'

'I can't believe that.'

'Honestly, Esther, that was exactly what he said,' Caroline insisted.

'Exactly?'

'Well ... almost. Near enough as to make no difference to his meaning. So here I am, back in London, and hating every minute of it,' she sighed.

'Thanks!'

'You know what I mean.'

'Mm. Well, why don't you go back to the cottage, talk things over with him?'

Caroline shrugged. 'I don't think we have anything left to say, we've already said far too much.'

'Surely anything is better than this misery?'

She shook her head firmly. 'I couldn't stand to become what I despise. And I would. You don't know how persuasive he can be. Each time he kissed me I just melted against him. He's just so—so devastating!'

'I believe it,' said Esther. 'The few photographs I've seen of him have obviously done him justice. I quite fancied him myself.'

'I don't think John would appreciate that. I——'

Someone walked unannounced into the room, and Esther's indignant expression lightened as she saw it was her brother. 'Nick! What are you doing here?'

'What a nice greeting!' he mocked, grinning

wickedly at the two of them before planting a kiss on each of their cheeks. 'My two favourite women.'

Unwillingly Caroline laughed at his spontaneous boyish charm. At twenty-seven, Nick Hall made no secret of the fact that he enjoyed life, and all it had to offer. He was relatively tall, dark-haired, with an olive skin and laughing blue eyes, very good-looking in a youthful way, and he had impeccable taste in clothing. The pin-striped suit and snowy white shirt he wore were evidence of that, and he wore them with a natural elegance that was eye-catching.

His sister frowned at him. 'What are you doing here this time of day?' she repeated.

'What a nag she is, Caroline!' He looked unperturbed. 'Brother-in-law John gave me the afternoon off.'

Esther pursed her lips disapprovingly. 'That means you asked him for the afternoon off under some pretext or other and he's too kind-hearted to refuse you. It also means he'll be late home himself,' she added darkly. Her husband and brother were in partnership together, although John seemed to deal with far more clients than Nick ever did.

'Calm down, sister dear.' He caressed one creamy cheek. 'John told me to tell you he'll be home at five-thirty as usual.'

'He knew you were coming here?'

Nick poured himself a cup of coffee, taking a cake off the plate. 'Of course he did. I'm not too busy at the moment, and I knew Caroline was going to be here this afternoon. I haven't seen you for ages,' he grinned at her.

'Don't exaggerate, Nick. We met at Hazel's party the other evening,' she reminded him.

'So we did, but that's not exactly the way I wanted to see you. How about coming out to dinner with me so that we can have a long chat together?'

'I don't think——' she began.

'Oh, that would be nice for you, Caroline,' interrupted Esther. 'You could try that restaurant John and I went to the other evening. It's——'

'Thank you, Esther,' her brother cut her off dryly. 'I think Caroline and I can make our own arrangements. I already have a restaurant in mind that I think Caroline would like.'

'No, really,' she shook her head. 'I'm not very good company at the moment, and I see no reason to spoil the evening for you too.'

'Oh, you wouldn't do that,' he denied. 'If you're feeling miserable I'm just the person to cheer you up.'

He probably was too. The four of them had had some uproarious times together in the past, although as he so rightly said, Nick and she hadn't seen too much of each other lately. He had always been a good friend to her, although that was no reason to inflict her company on him.

'I hope you don't mind if I still refuse, Nick. I would accept, but I'm not sure whether I'll be leaving town again soon.' Now why had she said that? She had no intention of going away so soon after her last escapade—at least she hadn't, until a few seconds ago. Her subconscious seemed to have made up her mind for her. And why not? She wanted to see André again, why deny it, and he was at the cottage.

'Does it have to be before we can get together?' Nick's frown mirrored his disappointment. 'I've been looking forward to seeing you.'

She laughed lightly at his flattery. 'You're seeing me now, silly. I don't have to go home just yet.'

She stayed another couple of hours, refusing Esther's offer of dinner as her father would be expecting her home. Now that she had made her mind up to return to the cottage and see André she was all eagerness to be on her way. He hadn't told her to leave, she had decided that alone, and so there was no reason why she shouldn't go back.

She had trouble pacifying her own conscience. Would André renew his pursuit of her, and if he did would she be strong enough to hold out against her own desire for him? Doubts began to enter her mind again, doubts for her own control. She had seen Esther's probing look at her sudden turn-about, after so recently declaring she couldn't possibly go back to see André to suddenly change her mind again. She had done the same thing constantly during the last few days, never knowing from one minute to the next what she wanted to do.

By the time her father returned home for dinner she had changed her mind half a dozen times. She saw his sharp look in her direction, and gave him a bright smile that only seemed to deepen his frown.

He paused over the eating of his meal, taking a sip of his wine. 'What's wrong, Caroline?'

She made an effort to look surprised by his question. 'Wrong?' she repeated. 'What could possibly be wrong?'

He sighed. 'That's what I'm asking you. And don't try to fob me off with any excuses, I want a straight answer.'

'I don't know what you're talking about,' she evaded. 'I'm feeling fine.'

'Oh, yes?' He gave a knowing nod of his head. 'That's why you don't eat any more and appear to have no further need of sleep, I suppose?'

'I'm sleeping and eating well.' Her cheeks filled with colour at her lie.

'Oh sure, you always eat like a bird and manage on two or three hours' sleep a night. Now come on, Caroline, this is your father you're talking to, not someone like Maggie or Esther who'll be put off by your feeble excuses. I'm not blind and I know you very well, no matter how much you may doubt that. And you aren't normal, you haven't been for some days now, ever since you returned from the cottage in fact.'

She evaded his eyes. 'Don't be silly. It's just the dull weather that's making me miserable, it's so depressing.'

'Ordinarily I would have believed you, but not this time. It's to do with Greg, isn't it? Something happened at the cottage that I should know about, something you're afraid to tell me.'

'It most certainly did not! I've done nothing to be ashamed of, nothing at all!' Her eyes glittered angrily. 'I left as soon as I found out who he is.'

'Who or what he is has nothing to do with the way you feel about him. How do you feel about him, Caroline, tell me that?'

She pushed the food around on her plate. 'How can I feel about him? He's Greg Fortnum, a rake, and totally immoral.'

Matt laughed. 'So? That doesn't stop women falling for him.'

'It does this one.'

'You aren't deceiving me, and you aren't deceiving yourself either, you fell for him in a big way,' he insisted.

'I did not!'

'Yes, you did, Caroline. I just hope you were sensible enough not to——'

'I was,' she said firmly.

'Good. I like Greg, but I will not have him taking advantage of my daughter. I wouldn't mind him as a son-in-law, but anything else is out of the question.'

'So is marriage.' This whole conversation was getting embarrassing. 'How would you feel about my going back to the cottage for a couple of days?' She waited breathlessly for his answer.

He shrugged. 'The same as I did last time. It's too

damned cold there this time of year for a hot-house plant like you. Other than that I have no objections.'

'And André?'

Matt frowned. 'What about him?'

'Won't you mind my staying with him?'

'But you won't be, he isn't there any longer. He left a couple of days ago for Europe and then on to the States. He called me on his way to the airport to thank me for the use of the cottage and its amenities—I think you came under the latter,' he added darkly. 'I remember I was quite annoyed about it at the time.'

CHAPTER EIGHT

HER evening out with Nick was not a success, as she
had known it wouldn't be. How could she laugh and
have fun when the man she loved believed her to be no
more than an 'amenity'? It had come as something of
a shock to her to realise that André was no longer even
in the same country as herself. While he had still been
at the cottage she had known she could change her
mind and return to him, but now he had gone to
Europe she knew she had no chance of seeing him.

She followed Nick back to their seats after their
dance together, brushing back her long hair. 'Phew,
there's a crowd in here tonight!'

Nick looked around at the bustle of people in the
nightclub. 'Mm,' he wrinkled his nose with distaste.
'It's become so fashionable here it's quite vulgar. If I'd
known I would never have brought you.'

'Never mind.' She touched his hand. 'I loved the
restaurant.' It had been Italian, and very exclusive.

He took a sip of the champagne he had insisted on
ordering. 'You're very quiet tonight, Caroline.'

'No, really, I'm fine.' And she was slightly better
than she had been during the week following her
father's revelation.

'Now come on, Caro, I know you and——'

'Don't call me that!' Her voice had risen shrilly and
her eyes darkened with anger. 'Don't call me that,
Nick,' she said more calmly. 'You never have before
and I—I don't like it.'

'Really?' He was watching her closely. 'It looked
the opposite to me.'

'You aren't in court now,' she told him sharply.

141

'Don't cross-question me.'

Nick laughed lightly. 'Now I know there's something wrong with you! And don't deny it again. We've never argued before, that's telling enough. Who else calls you Caro?' he asked shrewdly.

'No one.' She averted her head.

'All right, who *used* to call you Caro?'

'Please, Nick,' she put a hand to her temple. 'I have a headache, would you mind if we left?'

'If I promise not to pursue the subject will you stay a little longer?'

She shook her head, her excuse a reality as she felt a throbbing at her temples. 'No. I really don't feel well.'

He stood up, signalling the waiter for Caroline's wrap. 'Okay, let's go.'

'I'm sorry to have ruined your evening,' she said once they were outside in the car. 'But I did warn you.'

'So you did,' he grinned. 'So, who's the man?'

She frowned. 'You said you wouldn't pursue the subject,' she reminded him.

'Only if you stayed a little longer—and you didn't. Now don't evade the subject any more. This is Nick, your almost-brother, you can tell me what's troubling you.'

She gave a wan smile. 'Several people seem to have used similar arguments lately.'

'My dear little sister for one,' he guessed correctly. 'I gather I interrupted your little tête-à-tête with her last week? From the looks she was giving me I would say I'd come in at altogether the wrong moment.'

'Possibly,' she admitted.

'I gather Esther got it out of you who this mystery man is? Although I doubt she'll tell me.'

'There's no mystery about Greg Fortnum, everyone seems to have heard of him.'

Nick gave a low whistle. 'Greg Fortnum, eh? So he's the man! But I thought he was involved with Lisa Young at the moment?'

Caroline stiffened. 'He may be,' she said jerkily. 'I really wouldn't know.'

'Oh damn!' Nick swore. 'That was a bit tactless of me. Of course you wouldn't know who his—who his—er—friend——' he stumbled over the words.

'If you mean lover, Nick, then say it. I'm well aware that Greg is a grown man and has an expertise in love-making that comes from actual physical experience and nothing else,' she told him tight-lipped.

'Oh—oh, I see. Well, that's all right, then.' He breathed a sigh of relief that his blunder had passed with relative ease. 'I didn't know you knew him. I've met him a couple of times—formidable sort of chap.'

'I lived with him for five days,' Caroline stated calmly, laughing at his surprised face. 'Not in sin, I might add,' she said merrily, going on to explain the real circumstances behind her stay with André.

'You make it all sound very innocent,' Nick probed. 'Was it?'

She blushed at his direct question. 'More or less,' she answered evasively.

'How much was more and how much was less?'

'Quite a lot of the more and not too much of the less,' Caroline admitted honestly. 'But I came away unscathed.'

'But not with your heart intact. At a guess I would say you lost quite a big chunk to him.'

'At a guess you would be right.'

'So where is he now? I can't imagine why he let a beauty like you escape him.'

'He's somewhere in Europe.'

'And you're seeing him when he gets back?' He stopped the car in the forecourt of her apartment block, switching off the engine before turning to look at her.

'Not as far as I know, in fact I would say a definite no. We parted—badly.'

He leant forward and kissed her softly on the lips. 'Never mind, love, you still have me. God, that's enough to depress any girl!'

Caroline laughed. 'Thank you for the evening, Nick, and the shoulder to cry on.'

'You didn't cry.'

'No, but no doubt I will when I get in. I seem to have done little else lately. I'll see you again soon,' and she kissed him on the cheek.

After her disastrous evening with Nick she thought it better not to inflict her company on her other friends until she had herself under control again. What had happened to the self-assured Caroline Rayner who a couple of weeks ago wouldn't have been affected by any man? What had happened to the cool, composed Caroline who had always faced trouble head on? She had retreated into a lovelorn shell of herself, that was what had happened to her! But she would fight this emotion, fight the power it had over her. She groaned inwardly every time she thought of André. She had fallen in love for the first time in her life, and she had fallen hard. It wouldn't be so easy to dismiss it.

She spent hours in her studio at the apartment, working on the portrait of André. This was more out of necessity than actually wanting to do it. It had been the same at the cottage; no matter what she started she ended up going to the half-finished canvas of André that she tried to ignore.

It was a good portrait, even she could see that, definitely her best work to date. Her memory hadn't forgotten the deep mahogany of his skin, or the deep drowning green of his eyes. Every strong character of his face was there to taunt her, every mockingly handsome line. Somehow his arrogance came out in the portrait; it was unintentional, and yet it was there.

Once again Caroline turned her back on those taunting green eyes that seemed to watch her so intently, throwing a cloth over it so that she couldn't feel him looking at her any longer. Damn the man! She would get him out of her system if it took a lifetime—and at the rate she was progressing that was exactly how long it was going to take.

She was sitting in the lounge when her father came home. He was later than usual, but she made no comment, continuing to watch the television programme although it wasn't really interesting enough to hold her attention.

'Good evening, Caroline,' he said pointedly. 'Or don't you even bother with polite greetings any more?'

'Good evening, Daddy,' she answered obediently, not even bothering to look up, her chin resting on her bent knees as she sat in the chair.

He slammed the door behind him and she looked up with a start. His face was grim as he looked down at her. 'At last I have your attention, even if I did have to nearly break the door down in the process! Don't you think it's about time you rejoined the land of the living? Personally I'm getting sick and tired of looking at your woebegone face.'

Caroline took her feet off the chair and stood up. 'I'm sorry,' she said dully. 'I'll go to my room.'

'You'll damn well sit down and listen to me!' her father exploded. He watched with satisfaction as she did as she was told, frowning at the way her denims hung loosely on her hips. 'Have you eaten dinner?'

'I wasn't hungry.'

'You never are nowadays. Now you'll have to snap out of this mood, Caroline. Pull yourself together. You've been walking around like a ghost for long enough. You don't go anywhere, you don't see anyone, you've dropped out of the social world altogether. It's just not good enough, and I mean to see it doesn't continue.'

'Oh, yes?' There wasn't a spark of interest in her voice. Her hair hung limp and lifeless and there was none of the normal glow to her blue eyes.

'Yes,' he told her firmly. 'Now you're going to sit and eat dinner with me and then we're going out.'

'We are?' She raised one eyebrow.

'We are.'

'Where?'

He shrugged out of his jacket. 'Babs is throwing one of her parties this evening.'

'But you don't like those sort of parties.'

'I know that,' he said impatiently. 'But if it's the only way to get you out I'm willing to go. Besides, I like Babs.'

'And she likes you too.'

Matt sighed. 'None of your matchmaking tonight, Caroline! Ever since you were six years old and you realised you didn't have a mother like all the other kids you've been trying to find me a wife. I don't need or want a wife, and it's a bit late to start thinking of a mother for you. Although you look as if you could do with one right now.'

She blushed, pushing back her hair from her eyes. 'What do you mean?'

'Look at the state of you!' He poured himself a stiff measure of whisky. 'You aren't taking care of yourself any more—I can't remember the last time I saw you put on make-up. And your hair looks as if it could do with a good brush.'

'It needs washing,' she said moodily.

'Then damn well wash it! Come on, Caroline, get up off your backside and move yourself. We leave in less than an hour and I'm certainly not taking you anywhere looking like that.'

'I don't want to go. I'm perfectly happy where I am.'

'I couldn't care less whether you are or whether you aren't, you're coming with me. Now go and wash your hair and I'll tell Maggie we're ready for dinner.'

'But, Daddy, I——'

'Do it, Caroline! I'm fast running out of patience where you're concerned. Our going out this evening is not for discussion, we're going and that's that. Now move!'

She moved. She knew her father when he was in this mood, and it didn't pay to argue with him. And just maybe he was right. She studied her pale face in the bathroom mirror. She *did* look a mess. Her hair hadn't been washed and given a good brush for days, and her skin needed a proper cleansing and a moisturiser before she attempted to put make-up on it.

Why was she doing this to herself? All right, so she loved André, but looking like this she hadn't a hope of winning him—if she should ever see him again, that was. This was what was depressing her the most. She had never met him socially in the past, so why should she start now? Everything she did seemed so futile, so unnecessary.

Her father opened the bathroom door, frowning at her still form. 'Move, Caroline,' he snapped. 'I have every intention of taking you with me, so there's no point in delaying. We're going, even if we don't get there until midnight.'

'I'm not very good company, Daddy.'

'So you can sit in the corner all evening—but you're still going.'

She sighed. 'Yes, Daddy.'

He hesitated a moment. 'There isn't—isn't anything you want to tell me, is there?'

'Like what?'

'Well ... You aren't ill or—anything?' He couldn't

quite meet her eyes.

'Ill?' She looked puzzled and then blushed as she realised what he meant. 'No, I'm not ill—in any way.'

Her father looked slightly abashed. 'I'm sorry, but I had to ask. I know you told me nothing like that happened, but you may have just been too embarrassed to tell me about it. After all, it's not usually something you discuss with your father.'

'Nothing happened, Daddy,' she repeated.

He gave a relieved smile. 'I'll see you in a few minutes, then.'

An hour or so later she looked more like the Caroline of old. Her hair had been washed and now swung in golden waves down her back and curled softly about her cheeks. Her gown was the first one she laid hands on, but it suited her anyway. It was a black chiffon, strapless, but fitted over her not inconsiderable bust to fall in an A-line to her slender ankles. Her skin glowed a golden tan from the summer months and except for her slightly shadowed eyes she looked a picture of beauty. Her loss of weight made her appear more slender than ever and emphasised the fullness of her breasts, but perhaps that wasn't such a bad thing in this gown.

Her father gave her hand a confident squeeze before they entered Babs' house, set in an exclusive part of London. 'You look beautiful, poppet,' he told her in a whisper.

She certainly felt better than she had done for days, and she felt grateful for her father's deliberate boost to her confidence. 'I'll be all right, Daddy. You have no need to worry about me.'

He gave a rueful smile. 'And just what do you think I've been doing the last few weeks?'

'Well, you don't have to do it any more. Every girl falls in love disastrously once in her life.'

'Mm, but it was my fault. I could have saved you

all this heartache just by telling you who he was in the first place. After our earlier conversation about him you wouldn't have stayed. I was being my usual arrogant self, hoping things would work out as I'd planned, that the two of you would like each other.'

Caroline turned to straighten his tie. 'Let's forget it, Daddy.' She put her hand through the crook of his arm. 'Let's go and face the throng.'

'Mm,' he murmured grumpily.

She laughed at the expression on his face. He usually refused to go to these parties, declaring they were almost like a free-for-all. There wouldn't be many of her own friends here tonight; Babs Lerner was her father's age and consequently so were most of her friends. But Caroline had always liked Babs, and as her father had said, she had once hoped to have her as a stepmother. But it was not to be.

She was still laughing at her father's bad humour when they entered the crowded lounge, and the first person she saw was André! A different André from the one she was used to, dressed formally in a cream suit and contrasting brown shirt. His hair was brushed back in the casual windswept style he favoured. Within seconds of her seeing him he had spotted her too, those green eyes narrowing as he looked at her.

The smile faded from Caroline's lips and her skin became pale under her make-up. And she had thought she would never meet him socially! Her first evening out for days and here he was. She clutched compulsively at her father's arm and saw him follow her fixed gaze, nodding his head politely in acknowledgment as he recognised André.

'Did you know he was going to be here?' she muttered angrily under her breath, dragging her eyes determinedly away from that mocking face.

'How the hell would I know that?'

She looked at him closely, noting the slight flush

to his cheeks. 'You did know, don't bother to deny it. I always know when you're lying, you're on the defensive.'

'I could just be on the defensive because I'm innocent,' he blustered, smiling politely at the people who greeted him.

'You're not,' she returned firmly. 'How could you do this to me?' she asked brokenly. 'And after just apologising to me!'

'Now don't cause a scene here.' He took a drink from a passing waiter, handing one to Caroline. 'Drink some of that, it will steady your nerves. I'll just go and find our hostess and say hello.'

'Oh, but——' before she could say any more he had gone, leaving her alone and at the mercy of her own thoughts. André was at this party and at any moment she could come face to face with him! She went cold at the thought of it. How could her father do this to her!

She sensed rather than heard him behind her, her whole body feeling the electricity of his presence. 'Caroline.' His voice was husky and low and she turned slowly to greet him, forcing a tight smile to her frozen lips.

'André.' she acknowledged.

He smiled. 'That's an improvement! The last time we met you vowed you would never call me André again.'

'Did I?' she returned brightly. 'I can't remember every conversation we had.' But she could, she could!

'I can,' he said tautly, watching her over the flame of his lighter as he lit a cigarette. 'You came here with Matt?'

She shrugged. 'You saw us come in together.'

'That wasn't what I asked. Did you come here with him?' he repeated harshly.

'Yes.'

'Have you been with him all the time you've been back?' he returned sharply, his stance one of challenge.

'Most of it. But I——'

'I see. So you went straight back to him like a frightened child. I frightened you at the cottage, because I wanted you and I promised nothing in return for your delectable body. So you came back to your old lover.'

She shook her head. 'You don't understand. He isn't——'

André stubbed his cigarette out viciously. 'I understand all right. I just wish I could get you out of my mind.'

'Let me explain——'

'Greg darling!' A tall brunette swayed her way over to his side and Caroline recognised her as Lisa Young, one of the best-known actresses in the world today. She pouted up at him. 'Can we leave now, Greg?'

'Maybe.' He was still watching Caroline.

'You did promise we wouldn't have to stay long,' she insisted.

Caroline watched the two of them together, thinking what a handsome couple they made. Lisa Young was tall, much taller than Caroline, her hair arranged in a glowing cap about her beautiful face. Her red silk gown showed up vividly, drawing attention to her— which was probably the desired effect, Caroline thought bitchily.

'Greg?' the actress put in pleadingly. 'Let's go now. I want to meet the others at the club.'

He looked at her with irritation. 'Can't you see I'm talking to someone, Lisa? Just wait a few minutes and we'll be on our way.'

Deep brown eyes looked Caroline up and down. 'Do I know you?' she asked icily.

'I doubt it,' Caroline returned just as coolly.

'You look vaguely familiar,' the actress said thoughtfully. '*Should* I know you?'

'No,' Caroline lied. That was all she needed, for this woman to blurt out just exactly who she was. She intended telling André herself, not have him angered anew by finding out from someone else.

'Oh well,' Lisa Young lost interest. 'My mistake.'

'Okay, Lisa, let's go.' André took hold of her elbow. 'Goodnight, Caroline.'

She watched them leave, only coming to an awareness of her surroundings when her father touched her arm. 'What's the matter?' He looked down at her white face with concern.

'André just left,' she said dully.

'I would have thought that would have pleased you.' He looked puzzled.

'He spoke to me before he left.' She suppressed a cold shiver, even though the room was warm. 'And Lisa Young.'

'Mm, he's been friends with her for quite some time now.' He took hold of her arm. 'Come and say hello to Babs, she asked after you.'

'I—I want to leave.' Caroline licked her dry lips.

Her father's hold on her tightened. 'You have no reason to do that if Greg's already left.'

'I—I——'

'We're not leaving, Caroline. I brought you up with better manners than that. Babs is your hostess and you haven't even spoken to her yet,' he said angrily.

'Oh, Daddy!' her eyes begged him.

'Remember where you are, Caroline,' he snapped. 'Remember *who* you are.'

'All right,' she sighed. 'You win. I'm being hysterical about this. Where's Babs?'

Matt gave a triumphant smile. The first shock of seeing André was beginning to wear off, perhaps now she could get on with the rest of her life. This meeting had been necessary to shake her out of her mood of despondency, and while he hadn't been sure of André being here this evening, he had had a pretty good idea.

There was dancing in the other room, and after greeting Babs, Caroline accepted an invitation from one of the younger men to dance. She had met Mike a couple of times before, he was the son of one of her father's business associates. After that she danced with several of the younger members of the party.

She realised her mistake in accepting one rather persistent young man as soon as he began to touch her bare back with his hot sweaty hands. He was an old acquaintance of hers, but he had obviously had too much to drink, and all her efforts to stop his fumbling caresses were to no avail. He seemed to have the strength and hands of half a dozen men in his inebriated state, and Caroline was becoming quite agitated when she felt him suddenly wrenched away from her.

She looked up into blazing green eyes, André's face white with the effort it took him to hold on to his temper. But his anger and the contempt she saw in his eyes didn't seem important right now, all that seemed to matter to her was that he had come back. André had come back to the party! And he was alone.

CHAPTER NINE

'Go and get yourself some black coffee, Danville,' André growled at the younger man. 'And stop making a nuisance of yourself!'

Richard Danville flushed in the face of this powerful man's unhidden anger. 'I didn't know I was stepping on any toes, Greg, old man,' he blustered. 'I thought you were pretty well tied up with the beautiful and demanding Lisa.'

'Well, now you know I'm not,' André told him between gritted teeth. 'Now go and get that coffee.'

Caroline waited until he had left before turning on André. 'Did you have to humiliate him like that?' Her blue eyes flashed her dislike.

André took a tight hold of her arm and led her away from the curious eyes that had been turned on them during that obviously heated exchange. Thank goodness her father hadn't seen it, he would not have been pleased. 'I would have done more than humiliate him if we weren't in such a public place, I would have beaten him to a pulp. How dare you allow him to paw you about like that? And where the hell is Matt to allow it to happen?'

'He's talking to Babs somewhere,' she said vaguely, watching his scowling face. He was furiously angry, of that there could be no doubt. And she was the cause of that anger, that was obvious too.

'Then he should be keeping a better eye on his property,' he rasped. 'Allowing that young kid to wander his hands all over you!' he added in disgust.

'I've known Richard for years,' Caroline snapped back angrily. 'He's just had too much to drink. He'll apologise the next time we meet.'

Green eyes narrowed as he looked down at her, narrowing even more as they slid appraisingly up and down her slender body. 'It's that damned dress you nearly have on,' he muttered savagely. 'No wonder half the men in the room can't take their eyes off you.'

'Only half the men?' she queried flippantly, wincing as his fingers tightened painfully on her arm.

'You ought to be locked up,' he groaned in her ear. 'Locked up where no one else can look at you but me. Come on,' he began to pull her roughly towards the door. 'We're leaving.'

Caroline came to an abrupt halt, uncaring of the renewed pain to her bare arm. 'I can't do that,' she said stubbornly. 'I came here with—with Matt.' Now was hardly the time to explain that Matt was her father, not here in the middle of a noisy party. 'I can't just leave without telling him where I'm going—or who I'm going with.'

'Caro,' he looked down at her, his eyes deepening with an emotion she thought she recognised as passion, but surely she must be mistaken. But he had called her Caro! 'I want to be alone with you,' he insisted.

'And I have to let Matt know I'm leaving. He'll be worried about me if I just disappear.'

'Okay, okay,' he gave in impatiently. 'Let's find him and then get out of here.'

'I'm not sure I want to leave, André.' She hung back. 'Not with you in this mood.'

'What mood?' he frowned.

'That mood,' she said pointedly. 'You're angry and annoyed about something, and I think I'm to be the whipping-post. What happened? Did Lisa Young not like you talking to me and turn awkward?'

His eyes narrowed to icy green slits. 'What are you talking about, Caroline? What does Lisa have to do with us?'

She arched her eyebrows. 'Everything, I would have thought. She's your latest girl-friend, isn't she?'

'She was,' he told her grimly. 'I'm not going to explain anything in the middle of this crowd. Matt's over there,' he nodded in the direction of the smaller sitting-room.

By the time they reached her father's side she was resigned to the fact that André meant her to leave with him, and no matter what obstacles she put in his way he would walk right over them.

'Matt,' he said deeply, and she saw her father's eyes widen as he saw the two of them together. 'Matt, Caroline is leaving with me.'

Her father excused himself from the crowd of people he had been talking to. 'Is she now?' he queried mildly. 'Caroline?' he shot her a keen glance. 'How do you feel about this?'

She glanced nervously at the stony-faced André. 'Well, I——' She licked her dry lips.

'She's leaving with me, Matt,' he said firmly.

Her father gave him a cool look. 'Caroline is perfectly capable of answering for herself.'

They both looked at her and she looked from one to the other of them, not quite knowing what to do. She wanted to go with André, and yet she feared his mood. 'I——'

'You don't have to go, Caroline,' her father put in gently. 'You came with me, you can leave with me.'

In that moment she came to perhaps the most important decision of her young life. All her life she had depended on her father—oh, they argued, but that was only natural between two people so much alike, but for all their differences of opinion it was to him she ran when she was in trouble or anything was worrying her. But she couldn't depend on him for ever, sooner or later she was going to have to stand on her own two feet. And now was as good a time as any to start.

'I'll go with André,' she said in a rush.

'All right,' her father nodded approval. 'As long as it's your own decision I have no objection.'

'Thanks!' André growled, obviously not pleased by the other man's attitude. But then he didn't know he was her father; once he knew that he would understand his feelings better.

She gave a wan smile to her father before she was literally dragged away. A quick thank-you to Babs and they left her house, André tersely requesting her address as he slammed the car into gear. The way that he drove she could only hope that all his anger would have been exhausted on the car before they reached her apartment, otherwise she was in for a very rough time of it.

She let them into the apartment with her own key; Maggie would have gone to bed hours ago. 'Would you like some coffee?' She put her evening bag down on the glass-topped table.

He was looking about him appreciatively. 'Nice place you have here,' he remarked. 'Paid for by Matt, no doubt,' he stated.

Caroline moved forward. 'André, about Matt, I——'

He frowned darkly. 'I didn't come here to talk about Matt.'

'But——'

'I don't want to hear it, Caroline!'

So it was back to Caroline now! 'It's important. He——'

'For God's sake!' he swore angrily. 'Don't you know when to leave a subject alone? Your relationship with Matt isn't something I care to discuss.'

'But it's our relationship that's so important,' she said desperately. 'Matt isn't——'

'Will you shut up, girl!' He pulled her against him, making her fully aware of his arousal. 'I want to make love to you, not listen to what Matt is or isn't.'

'Oh, please, André,' she cried. 'Just let me explain.'

'No.' His mouth tightened. 'The only thing I want you to do right now is kiss me. Kiss me as if your life depended on it,' he ordered. 'Because I think mine just may do.'

His dark head bent and his lips claimed hers, forcing her mouth open to receive him. He devoured her with his mouth, making her forget all her carefully rehearsed explanations, all her excuses for her unforgivable lies, and think only of him and the way his hands caressed her body and his lips evoked pleasure almost too much to bear.

He moved his head slightly to look down at her with passion-filled eyes, her body soft and pliant in his hands. 'I'm hungry for you, Caro,' he groaned, his voice husky with emotion. 'Just hungry for you!'

Her body moved against him of its own volition and she felt him quiver against her. She fitted against him as if they were made to join together, and her hands ran lovingly through his thick vibrant hair.

Those tantalising lips ran down the side of her neck and across her bare shoulders. She groaned against him as his mouth fired her senses aflame, feeling herself lowered gently on to the sofa, her eyes pleading for his return as he moved across the room to turn off the lights, their only illumination now coming from the not too bright moon.

André returned to her side, his jacket tossed carelessly aside, his shirt completely unbuttoned. He laid his long length beside her, his bare chest inciting her to more fevered caresses as their lips met and clung once more.

'God, you're beautiful!' he moaned, his face buried in her long blonde hair. 'I've thought of no one but you since you left the cottage, thought of nothing but the last time I held you in my arms. And I've cursed

Sylvia a thousand times for her interruption. If she hadn't called me at that moment then all this could have been mine.' His lips travelled across the creamy expanse of skin visible above her strapless dress, his hands moving across her back to the zip with an expertise she hardly recognised.

She felt the slight coolness of the zip travelling down and began to squirm in his arm. 'Please, André, don't do that.'

He ignored her half-hearted plea, ravaging the nakedness of her breasts until she forgot her protests and gave herself up to the heated emotions of her own body, emotions that only his full possession of her would assuage.

'You shouldn't have left me,' came his husky mutterings. 'We could have stayed together at the cottage for days, weeks, as long as it pleased us to. You knew this was inevitable, that I would have to possess you in the end, so why make us wait, why make us both suffer this torment?'

'I didn't, André.' Her eyes were violet with passion. 'You frightened me, and you rushed me.'

He gave a throaty chuckle. 'And what do you think I'm doing now if I'm not rushing you? This time I'm not taking no for an answer.'

She looked at him below lowered lids. 'Who said I was going to say no?' she asked softly.

Again he chuckled. 'And I said you had nothing to offer a man! You can give me all——'

The sound of another key entering the lock stopped him in mid-sentence, and guessing it was her father she hastily pulled her gown back up, attempting to do up the zip and failing miserably in her panic. The two of them blinked painfully as the lights blazed on.

Shock was written all over her father's face as he looked at them, and Caroline could only imagine the sight they must look. 'Good God!' he muttered indistinctly. 'Just what do you think you're doing?' he looked at the other man questioningly.

André stood up and she saw the chaos her caressing hands had wrought to his styled hair, making him more rakishly attractive than ever. 'What are you doing here, Matt?' he asked coldly, calmly buttoning his shirt and tucking it back in the waistband of his trousers.

'I live here,' Matt informed him just as coolly.

'You *what*?' The question was directed at Matt, but he was looking at Caroline.

'I live here.' Matt strolled further into the room. 'This is my apartment.' He was only making the situation worse in his anger.

Green eyes blazed down at her. 'You little bitch!' André picked up his jacket and marched to the door. 'My God!' he muttered. 'You first class little bitch!' he repeated, the door slamming on his exit.

'Oh, Daddy!' She looked at him through tear-washed eyes, her face blanching as she saw him slowly sink to the floor.

Her face was pale as she sat in the waiting-room of this highly clinical hospital. She felt so useless sitting here, felt as if she should be doing something, anything but just waiting here.

Her father had been rushed to hospital over an hour ago, Caroline managing in her complete panic to realise that an ambulance had to be called and expert medical treatment given to her father if he were to live.

She could tell by his rasping breathing and the blueness about his lips that this was no ordinary faint. Something was seriously wrong, so wrong that she hadn't been able to wake him. He was completely unconscious, and on getting him to the emergency department of this busy hospital the numerous staff had rushed about trying to see what could be done for him.

So here she still sat, an hour later, feeling as if an axe were hovering above her head. Would her father live or die?—it was that serious, she knew that. No one seemed prepared to tell her anything at the moment, probably because there was nothing they could tell her yet.

She looked up hopefully as another nurse walked past the door, but slumped down again in her chair as she went straight past. Why didn't they tell her something, *anything*? She felt sick and faint at the same time, her fear for her father deep-rooted. He had to live, he just had to!

She could hear someone walking down that long white corridor towards her, her face suddenly white, her eyes deeply violet. Would it be good news or—or bad? Her heart leapt as the door swung open and a man entered.

'Uncle David!' She sprang to her feet, tears of relief at seeing a familiar face streaming down her cheeks. She ran into his arms. 'Oh, Uncle David,' she choked, her body racked by deep sobs now.

He let her cry for several minutes longer, a man in his mid-fifties, his iron-grey hair brushed back from his lined face. Tall and distinguished-looking in his dark grey suit, David Clarke had been a family friend throughout the whole of her childhood. He had been the heart specialist called in during her mother's illness.

She looked up at him sharply. He was a heart specialist! 'Uncle David?' her voice quivered. 'Daddy?' she squeaked.

His hands tightened on her arms, shaking her gently at the hysteria in her voice. 'I've just been in to see him. He's had a heart attack, but he's going to be fine.'

'Thank God for that!' She collapsed against him. 'Oh, thank God!' she cried silently now.

'He's going to be fine,' he repeated. 'But it's going to be a long struggle. Nothing will ever be the same again.'

Caroline smiled up at him brightly. 'As long as he's all right I don't care what we have to do.'

'When I say nothing will ever be the same, that's exactly what I mean,' he frowned. 'Your father needs complete rest, away from any worries whatsoever.'

'And he'll have one,' she promised. 'Can I see him now?' she asked anxiously.

David pushed her firmly down into a chair. 'Now just sit there and listen to me for a moment. Your father is sleeping right now anyway, so a couple of minutes more won't make any difference to him. I want you to understand the seriousness of the situation. Matt——'

'I understand how serious it is,' she told him brokenly. 'I was with him when it happened, remember?'

'I know.' He sat down beside her, gently holding her hand. 'And I realise it must have been distressing for you. But it could have happened at any time. I warned Matt time and time again that he had to take things easy, but he always had too much to do, too many people to see. And now he's flat on his back in a hospital bed, as I warned him he would be.'

Her eyes opened wide. 'You—you warned him?'

'Numerous times during the last couple of years,' he sighed. 'But he didn't even have the time to listen to me.' He shook his head.

Caroline felt a cold chill run up her spine, looking dazedly at her hand held in his. 'Are you——' her voice cracked. 'Are you telling me that Daddy *knew* he had a heart condition?'

David's look could only be described as sympathetic. 'He knew, Caroline,' he told her gently. 'He knew that if he didn't slow down or hand over the reins of Rayner Enterprises to someone else, then this was going to happen sooner or later. He took a gamble on it being later—and lost.'

Her shock at what David was telling her was almost too much to bear. Her father had known of his illness, and yet he had carried on as normal, had not even told her! 'I—I don't believe it.'

'Believe it, Caroline. And believe me when I say I'm sorry it had to be like this. Matt will have no choice now, the firm will have to go. There's no way he can go back to living under that pressure almost a hundred per cent of the time.'

'He doesn't have to work, he doesn't need the money, he already has more than he knows what to do with.'

'It isn't the money, that isn't why he wanted to carry on working. The firm is *him*, he couldn't bear to see it sold to someone who perhaps wouldn't see things his way, or who would break up the company into smaller subsidiaries. Can you imagine what it would do to him to see his company, his life's work, fall about him in ruins? Because that's what will happen if he doesn't get somebody competent to take over.'

'But he has his assistant John Buck, he could take over under Daddy's guidance.'

He shook his head. 'That could only ever be a temporary measure, not a long-term one. It all comes back to the fact that Matt just can't carry on as he has been.' He straightened. 'I think that's enough about that now. I'm sure you're anxious to see him.'

The shock of her father's serious illness and the fact that he had kept it from her for the last two years stayed with Caroline over the next few weeks. He had been gravely ill for several days, only being removed from the intensive care unit to a private room after several days of specialised nursing, when at times his life had hung in the balance.

There had been as little publicity about his illness as possible, at his own request, the worldwide knowledge of his collapse possibly causing a recession to his company shares, which he didn't want. Nevertheless, several of his really close business colleagues were informed, and André was one of them.

It had been an added shock when opening the telegrams they had received to find one from him. It had been sent from America, but the good wishes for her father's recovery were obviously sincerely meant, and she had felt tearful after reading it.

She had thought of him as little as possible during the last few weeks, trying in vain to force out of her memory thoughts of their last meeting together. Her father's interruption had perhaps stopped her doing something she would later have regretted, but she also had to face the fact that the situation her father had come in on had been the cause of his collapse. Uncle David had insisted that no one thing had set it off, but a coming together of several worries over the last few months, but this didn't really help ease her conscience.

'Caroline!' Her father's voice rang out sharply now and she turned to look at him. How dear to her he was, lying there propped up by several pillows, his face having slowly lost that greyness she had found so frightening.

She smiled at him now, and moved to his side. 'Yes, Daddy?' she asked softly. The strain of the last few weeks had taken their toll on her too, leaving her thin and pale, and the nervous movements of her hands were almost second nature.

He patted the bed for her to sit down beside him. 'I think it's time we talked, Caroline,' he said seriously.

'Talk?' She evaded his eyes. 'But we've done nothing else during the last few weeks! This is your first day home, surely we can think of something better to do than talk.'

Matt looked wryly at the neatly made-up bed around him. 'I can't do much else at the moment *except* talk, and although we talked a lot while I was in hospital we didn't really discuss the subject most on both our minds.'

Caroline attempted a light laugh. 'I can't imagine what you mean, Daddy. We seem to have covered every conceivable subject.'

He patted her hand. 'I know that, you've been very good, visiting me at the hospital a couple of hours each day. Don't think I haven't appreciated it.'

'Don't be so silly!' She looked scandalised. 'You're my father, where else would I be but at your side? Besides,' she added teasingly, 'I had nothing else to do.'

'Thanks!' he laughed. 'But that isn't strictly true. I'm sure Esther has been plaguing you to go out to different places with her during your stay there.'

Esther and John had insisted she move in with them during her father's illness, and although she had refused at first, they had persisted with their invitation until her father had joined in the argument for her to stay with them. As he wasn't to be distressed in any way she had agreed in the end, and she had to admit that it had been the wisest thing to do. Esther and John had not intruded on her worry for her father, but they had always been there when she felt like company.

She smiled. 'Only because you told her to,' she answered him. 'I'm perfectly well aware that you telephoned Esther and told her to take me out.'

He sighed. 'You're too damned clever for your own good. Yes, I asked her to get you out. You're so pale, Caroline. You don't look well. Some of the times you visited me you looked as if you should have been the one in the bed. So how about that talk now?'

Caroline got up and moved away to look out of the huge window that overlooked the river. 'What do you want to talk about?' She couldn't look at him.

'I think André would be as good a thing as any,' he suggested gently.

'André?' she questioned sharply. 'The name is Greg.'

'His name is André,' he said equally firmly. 'And from now on that's exactly what I intend to call him.'

She turned on him fiercely. 'When you accuse us both of causing your attack?' She shook her head. 'You have no need to do that, Daddy. I know who was to blame for that, and I——'

'*You* will kindly shut up while I put you right on several points,' he interrupted shortly. 'Firstly, you did nothing to bring on my attack. I managed that quite well on my own, thank you. I've been overworking, and I suppose the fact that I knew about the weak ticker didn't really help me. Secondly, I want you to know that it was only concern for your future that made me keep introducing you to eligible bachelors. It was in the hope that one of them might be the one for you and would look after you if anything happened to me.'

'Oh, Daddy!'

'Don't look like that, poppet. I'm not invincible, this illness has proved that, and I wanted to be sure of your happiness in the event of that happening.'

'And André?'

Now it was her father's turn to look away. 'Yes— André. Now in his case I wasn't being strictly unselfish.'

'I thought not,' she said dryly.

He cleared his throat noisily. 'I may be your father, Caroline, but I'm also the owner of a large and prosperous firm. André happens to be the shrewdest business man I know, and if Rayner Enterprises belonged to him he would run it as it should be run.'

'Rayner Enterprises isn't for sale,' she said primly.

'True,' he agreed. 'But I wouldn't have minded

making a gift of it to my daughter and son-in-law.'

'So that's what it was all about!' Her mouth tightened angrily. 'No wonder you didn't come and get me from the cottage! We played right into your hands by both insisting on staying there. How you must have enjoyed yourself!'

'It was convenient, that was all. As you may have already gathered, André was no more interested in marriage than you were. He didn't want to meet you either, he used going to the cottage to rest as an excuse for not coming here for that weekend. But I hoped that once you had met you would be attracted to each other. After all, you're both handsome specimens.'

'That doesn't necessarily induce attraction.'

'I realise that. But in this case it did. You were attracted from the first—admit it.' He looked at her hopefully.

She shook her head, smiling at his disappointment. 'Not from the first,' she denied. 'That came later. I suppose I was always aware of him as a sensually attractive man, but he annoyed me so much at first that I didn't have time to notice anything else.'

'You do understand why I would have liked him to have Rayner Enterprises? He would run it successfully,' he said with certainty.

'No doubt. So why not just sell it to him if you feel this way? He has enough money to buy it, there's no need to marry me off to him.'

Matt looked disgruntled. 'I wanted to keep it in the family.'

'In other words you still wanted to have a say in the running of it even though it no longer belonged to you.' She gave a harsh laugh. 'No wonder you changed from introducing me to men like Anthony, he would never have been able to cope with the firm.'

'Much too weak,' he agreed.

'And André is much too strong a personality to allow you to interfere in the running of any business he owned. You should have known that, Daddy. It just wouldn't have worked out the way you wanted it.'

'It would if he had fallen in love with you. I've been on the receiving end of your wheedling, remember? I know how you can twist people who love you around your little finger.'

Caroline made a scoffing noise. 'Not someone like André. Men like him don't fall in love, they have affairs.' She should know, she had so nearly begun one with him herself. A few more minutes alone with him and she would have been totally committed, both in body and soul.

'It's this ruse of yours that gave him the wrong impression about you. I really thought when you left the party together that you'd told him the truth,' he sighed. 'When I came in and André reacted so violently I realised I'd been mistaken. He was furious, Caroline. He really thought you'd brought him back to the apartment of your middle-aged lover.'

She rubbed her hands nervously. 'He wouldn't listen to me. I tried to explain, but he wouldn't listen!'

'All right, don't upset yourself. His cable didn't say when he would be back from the States, but I think you should see him and explain as soon as he returns.'

Caroline looked taken aback. 'I couldn't—I can't see him again! Not after the names he called me.'

'They were mild compared with what he could have called you. In the same situation I would have probably gone to town on you.'

She sighed. 'He probably would have done too if he hadn't been quite so boilingly angry.'

'Well, I'm glad you're going out with your friends this evening. An evening out at one of the clubs is just what you need.'

'You know I don't want to go. I only agreed to it because you kept pushing me. This is your first evening home, I wanted to stay with you.' Her eyes were pleading.

'You're going out. Go to your room and get yourself ready.' Matt sank down below the covers. 'I feel like a rest. It's amazing how easily tired I get, and we have been talking quite a while.'

Instantly she was at his side. 'How thoughtless of me! Now lie back and rest and I'll get you——'

'You won't get me anything. Maggie's here, she's just dying to fuss around me.'

'But I——'

'Please, Caroline! I don't have the strength to argue with you. You're taking unfair advantage of my weakness.'

'All right, I'll go. But make sure you do rest, none of this sneaking looks at business files as you were in hospital until that young nurse caught you.'

He chuckled. 'Believe me, I'm going to rest.'

CHAPTER TEN

CAROLINE was spending the evening with Esther, John, and Nick, something she hadn't done for some time. The club was crowded as usual, but Nick had little trouble finding them a table, laughingly telling them that he was a friend of the management, and it seemed to be true from the preferential treatment they received.

She enjoyed the light bantering that made up the evening, using up masses of energy as she danced almost every dance. She was much in demand by the two men, as Esther cried off dancing.

'Anything wrong?' Caroline asked her during a quiet moment.

Esther gave a glowing smile. 'Everything's fine. You'll have to excuse John if he gets slightly merry this evening. I only told him a couple of hours ago that he's going to be a father.'

'Really? That's wonderful!'

The four of them 'wet the baby's head' so much that night that Caroline felt quite tipsy by the time she let herself into the apartment. She was totally unprepared for the sight that met her eyes.

'André!' She stepped back, coming up against the closed door.

He was just as attractive as ever, more tanned and virile-looking, but that was probably from the American sun. He was dressed casually in denims and a roll-necked sweater that moulded to his muscled shoulders and flat stomach. 'Caroline,' he nodded arrogantly.

Taking a deep breath, she moved further into the room, throwing her wrap and evening bag on to the side table. 'When did you arrive?' She straightened her hair in front of the mirror.

'A couple of hours after you left to meet your friends, I believe,' he remarked tautly, watching her movements through narrowed eyes.

'Why are you still here?' she asked rudely, completely unnerved by his unexpected presence in her own home. Was nowhere safe from him?

'Not in the hope of seeing you, I can assure you,' he retorted equally cuttingly. 'Matt's just fallen asleep. I came out here to collect my jacket and then leave.'

'I didn't think you were about to steal the family silver,' Caroline told him sarcastically. 'Greg Fortnum has no need of other people's silver.'

'For God's sake, what's this hang-up you have about my name?' André demanded impatiently.

'Hang-up? I don't have a hang-up about it. You lied to me, deliberately deceived me.'

'Okay, so I lied, but only to get a little peace and quiet.' He ran an agitated hand through his thick dark hair. 'How the hell Matt can still stand to have you about after finding us together I can't imagine! I would have throttled you if the positions had been reversed.'

'And instead he collapsed with a heart attack,' she put in quietly.

'He did *what*?'

'You heard me. Did it never occur to you that we might have been the reason for his attack—you, me, and the situation he found us in? Didn't you realise I would have followed you and explained if something hadn't happened to stop me?'

'How the hell would I know? As far as I was concerned we had nothing left to say to one another. You mean Matt collapsed after I'd left?'

She nodded confirmation. For the past few weeks she had kept her emotions firmly in check, not wishing to distress her father any more than necessary. But with André she felt her defences crumble away and the misery she had held back for so long threatened to overflow.

Her shoulders shook as she cried. 'Oh, André!' she muttered miserably. 'It was terrible. You can't imagine how I felt when I saw him sink to the ground, that ghastly blueness about his lips.'

'We weren't to blame for the attack.' He sounded preoccupied, her tears not moving him at all. 'I've just had a long chat with Matt, and he didn't sound as if he blamed me.'

Caroline sniffed inelegantly. 'He wouldn't do that, he isn't the type of person to point fingers.'

'Matt's a brutally honest person, and if he blamed me at all he would have said so. As it turned out we didn't mention you at all.'

Her eyes widened. 'You—you didn't?' So her father hadn't told him the truth. He was leaving that to her, trusting her to be brave enough to reveal the truth about their living together. She wasn't sure she was up to it.

'Except for Matt to tell me you'd gone out with friends. I find it incredible that he still bothers with you. You left him to stay with a stranger in a remote cottage, he walks in on a very heated moment in that stranger's arms, and then you proceed to leave him alone on his first evening home from hospital to go out with your own friends.'

'Da he insisted I go, I didn't want to go.'

'You don't exactly look as if you sat miserably in the corner all night. You're ever so slightly drunk.'

'I'm not. I—we've been wetting the baby's head.'

His look sharpened. 'Baby?'

She sighed at the suspicion in his face. 'Not mine, a close friend is expecting her first child.'

'Mm,' he frowned darkly. 'Well, I think I should be

on my way now. I don't want to help you make Matt any more jealous than he needs to be, not in his condition.'

'André, I—I——'

'Yes?' he asked sharply, shrugging his shoulders into the dark leather jacket he had left thrown across an armchair. Caroline didn't think Maggie would appreciate his untidiness.

'I have something to—to tell you.' Now it had come to it she really felt nervous. André wasn't the easiest of people to sit down and talk to, and what she had to tell him wasn't going to please him. She had taken her deceit a lot further than he had, hadn't owned up to it, and now she felt only nervousness instead of the elation she had planned.

He straightened the collar of his jacket. 'And what is that?'

He sounded so uninterested that she felt her temper rising. 'It's important,' she insisted, delaying the dreaded moment for as long as possible.

André sighed. 'It's late, Caroline, and I'm not in the best of tempers. Say what you have to say and then I can get home. I only flew in from the States earlier today.'

'I—— It isn't easy.'

He sighed again. 'Nothing is ever straightforward where you're concerned, I've found.'

'If you're going to be nasty ...' What a coward she was! Why didn't she just get it over with?

'Aren't I always?' he taunted.

'Yes,' she snapped, her tenseness making her sharper with him than she intended. 'I'm—— Matt isn't my—my lover,' she saw his disbelieving look and this spurred her on. 'And my name isn't Rawlings, you were right when you suspected it wasn't.' She took a deep breath. 'My name is Rayner, and Matt is my father.'

It had all come out in a rush and she could see his face becoming darker with anger at each word. If she had thought she had seen him angry before she now knew differently. His green eyes blazed down at her and his face was pale with anger, a whiteness about his mouth that pointed to him almost being out of control.

'André?' she looked at him anxiously.

He still remained silent, moving away to the other side of the room as if he might strike her if he didn't do so. 'My God!' he finally muttered. 'Matt's daughter!'

'I—You—Yes!' What else could she say?

Suddenly he turned on her, his eyes accusing. 'I should have realised, should have guessed you were his spoilt little daughter. How could I have been so blind, so damned stupid!'

'You weren't to know. It was your attitude that annoyed me to start with, the way you had formed an opinion of me without even knowing me, so I lied about my name.'

His mouth turned back in a sneer. 'Don't add insult to injury. Matt made no secret of his matrimonial plans concerning his daughter and myself, and I was equally voluble about my dislike of such plans. So he sent you to the cottage, knowing full well I was going there.'

'He did no such thing!' she said indignantly.

'All right, maybe you decided that all by yourself. But you were there, no matter how it came about. You set out from the first to attract me—and don't deny it, because you know it's true.'

It was true, but not in the way he was implying. 'I don't deny it, but——'

'Good God!' he swore. 'And I fell right into your trap. No wonder Matt warned me off—he hoped to make me more interested in you.' He gave a bitter laugh. 'He didn't need to do that, I found you very attractive already.'

'You're wrong, André. Please believe me.'

'No, *you* believe me, Caroline. I wouldn't marry you under any circumstances. I find you sexually attractive and exciting, but I wouldn't marry you. Matt may be able to give you a lot with his money, but he isn't giving you me. He doesn't have anything I want that badly, and neither do you.'

She had expected anger from him, but not this hatred and disgust. 'Oh, André . . .' Tears gathered in her limpid eyes.

'You knew who I was all the time,' he said scathingly. 'So you can drop the act now, no one's impressed, especially me. I have no particular wish to see you ever again.'

'Oh, please——'

'Goodbye, Miss Rayner,' he said chillingly.

Caroline looked much healthier for her prolonged stay in Barbados; long weeks of doing nothing but laze in the hot sun had agreed with her. Her skin glowed with a golden hue that was due entirely to the healthy tan she had acquired, and although still far too slender she no longer had those unhappy shadows in her eyes.

Her father was the main cause of that, giving her back the confidence she had lost at André's ruthless hands. He had also at last managed to convince her that she was in no way responsible for his illness, blaming himself totally for not heeding David Clarke's expert advice.

He was still in Barbados, accompanied by the faithful Maggie, and was likely to stay there for the rest of his life. They had all moved out there as soon as her father was well enough to fly, and her father had decided now was the right time to sell Rayner Enterprises. His health would always be a fragile thing and so there was only one thing left to do, sell his prosperous business.

And so Caroline was here in London to meet the prospective buyer and take him back to the villa with her. There had been quite a few people interested in the company, but her father seemed to consider this one the most suitable, the one most likely to keep things as they were, and retain the same staff. She had at first refused to come here, not understanding the need for her actually to come here in person to meet this man. But her father had insisted that in business it was the personal touch that mattered. She had agreed to come in the end, mainly because she also wanted to do some shopping.

The apartment seemed curiously empty without the presence of Maggie and her father, rather ominous in a way. She had been back two days now and would meet the man at the airport on their way to the villa. She had a complete new wardrobe for her trouble, but she would still be glad to get back to Barbados. So far she had seen nothing of André during her visit—and she intended for things to remain that way.

She sighed, turning away from her reflection in the full-length mirror. Just the thought of André was enough to reduce her to misery. The last few months had done nothing to lessen her feelings towards him, if anything they were stronger. But what was the good of even thinking about him, he didn't even want to see her again.

She glanced at her watch; almost time for her to leave for the airport and meet Mr Andrews. She had never met the man, but her father assured her that she would be recognised. He had jokingly told her that she was beautiful enough for her face to be well known.

She was a picture of cool self-confidence as she waited in the first-class lounge, the brown tailored suit and cream blouse emphasising her slenderness. She would have to change before they reached Barbados, but the weather in England wasn't yet warm enough to merit a summer dress.

'Are you ready to leave, Caroline?' enquired that familiar taunting voice.

Her skin pale she turned to face him. She had thought she was imagining things when she heard that voice, but no, it was definitely André before her. He hadn't changed at all, perhaps slightly leaner than she remembered, but otherwise exactly the same, the same taunting quirk to his mouth and mockery for her in those green eyes. He was dressed in a dark grey business suit and white shirt, looking much more the successful business man she knew him to be.

'André . . .' she trailed off faintly.

'That's right.' He indicated her handbag lying on the chair behind her. 'Is that all you have with you?'

'I—Yes.' She couldn't take her eyes off him, he was the last person she had expected to see.

He quirked an eyebrow at her. 'We're leaving. I've arranged for your cases to be taken off the flight. Come on!' He looked at her impatiently.

Caroline moved jerkily, her eyes dazed. 'I—but I can't leave. I'm—I'm meeting someone.'

'I know—me.' He pushed her bag into her hands and taking her arm in a firm grip he led her out of the waiting-room and out of the airport.

She waited until he had seated her comfortably in the car before saying anything further, the shock of seeing him again making her feel so confused she couldn't think straight. She finally gathered her wits together enough to make some comment. 'You?' she squeaked. 'But your name isn't Andrews.'

His mouth lifted at the corners as he secured her safety belt for her. 'Very observant, Caroline.'

'Then what did you mean? Look, I can't be here with you. My father is expecting——'

'Me,' he repeated. 'I'm Mr Andrews.'

'But you can't be,' she said desperately.

'Oh, but I am. Now just calm down, all will be explained to you in due time. Until then I suggest you just settle back and enjoy the scenery.'

'I'm not enjoying this at all,' she told him crossly. 'I want my explanation now.'

'Then you can just want, because you aren't going to get one now. I'm not your father, and I won't be swayed by a little of your pouting.'

He remained stubborn throughout the whole of their journey, insisting she watch the scenery and not worry so much. The one thing that really annoyed her was that her father had managed to trick her once again. He had known she didn't want to see André, had known that she would never willingly meet him again, and so he had engineered this little plan to dupe her. She would have a few things to say to him when she saw him again. When she saw him again! She had no idea when that would be.

It soon became clear to her where their final destination was going to be. 'We're going to the cottage.' It was a statement, not a question.

'You're very astute today, Caroline.'

'And you're your usual mocking self,' she retorted crossly. 'Why are we going to the cottage? And why are you masquerading as Mr Andrews?'

'We aren't there yet. I told you I wouldn't answer any questions until then, that still stands. Now just be patient a little longer. I realise patience isn't one of your virtues, but ...'

'Ooh, you're so damned annoying!'

'You already know my numerous faults, Caro— perhaps that's as well in the circumstances.'

'Circumstances?' she echoed sharply.

'You'll have to wait for explanations.'

She just glared at him furiously, knowing that inflexibility of old—and knowing he would remain adamant. By the time they reached the cottage she was boilingly angry—angry with her father, angry with André, and most of all angry with herself for even allowing him to get her into his car. She should have flatly refused to go anywhere with him, and she would have done if he hadn't been so domineering, so bossy, so——

'We've arrived, Caroline,' André interrupted her thoughts, getting out of the car and coming round to open her door for her.

She got out woodenly, following him as he unlocked the door and led the way through to the lounge. Although almost nine o'clock in the evening it was still light outside, the summer nights staying light until well after ten o'clock.

André looked about him appreciatively. 'It hasn't changed,' he said with satisfaction.

'Did you expect it to have done?' she snapped.

He shrugged, turning to look at her. 'I couldn't be sure, it's almost six months since we were last here.'

'And it doesn't seem a day too long.' She turned up her nose haughtily. 'Now if you've finished this trip down memory lane, perhaps we could leave. I have to get a flight back to Barbados.'

'You aren't going anywhere.' He watched her through narrowed eyes. 'Not until we've spoken together like reasonable adults, which doesn't seem to be all that easy between the two of us.'

'I would say it was impossible!'

He shook his head. 'If only you didn't keep losing your temper——'

'*Me* lose my temper? You're a fine one to talk! I seem to remember that on the last two occasions we've met it's been *you* who's lost their temper.'

'With good reason,' he returned abruptly.

'Like hell it was! It was your damned arrogance.'

'It appears to me,' his voice was dangerously soft, 'that you do altogether too much swearing and cursing. It isn't at all ladylike.'

Caroline turned away in disgust. 'You're beginning to sound like Daddy!'

'That isn't surprising, I probably feel like him at the moment. You need a good hiding, Caroline.'

'So you keep telling me. So let's have the reason for your alias this time, *Mr Andrews*.'

'One of these days ...' he muttered. 'God, you're an antagonising little wretch at times.' He ran a hand through his thick dark hair. 'I used the name Andrews because your father and I thought you wouldn't meet me if you knew who I actually was.'

'You both thought right. So you want Daddy's firm?'

'That's right.'

'So?' she frowned. 'You don't need my approval for that, in fact you don't need me here at all.'

He took a step towards her. 'Oh, but I do, Caro. I need you very much.' His voice had lowered caressingly.

She looked at him sharply, at last beginning to realise the reason behind this meeting. And the realisation brought pain to her heart. 'God, I thought my father could be a cold-hearted swine at times, but you can be a bastard, a first-class bastard!'

His green eyes narrowed to slits. 'What are you talking about now?'

'Have you decided to take the carrot my father has so temptingly been dangling in front of you? Why not? After all, you're a business man, you know a good deal when you see one. Why bother to buy something that can be given to you if you just marry the spoilt little daughter?' She was well into her tirade by now. 'Well, there's one little thing wrong with that plan—me. I'm not agreeable. Do you understand that?'

The whiteness about his lips and his dark brows

drawn together over glittering eyes were evidence of his own anger. 'You really believe I would marry you just to get my hands on Matt's company?'

'Why not? Daddy's old-fashioned about these things, nothing less than marriage would satisfy him. He would probably just hand you his company if you married me—he almost came up here with a shotgun and forced you to marry me the last time we were here together.'

'I bought your father's company two months ago,' he stated calmly. 'I also made your father a member of the board. And I paid the full price for it.'

Caroline looked at him dazedly. 'You—you did?'

He nodded. 'I did. Now do I merit an apology?'

'I—I don't know, I don't know anything any more. Wh-what am I doing here? Why did you bring me here?'

'I already told you that. I need you.'

'But you have Daddy's company, and the last time we spoke together you told me you didn't want to see me again.'

'You know the reason for that. You're a Rayner, that takes some getting used to, especially after the things I'd accused you of being.' He gave a grim smile. 'I think I've finally come to terms with the fact that you're Matt's daughter.'

'And?'

'And I've been in contact with him pretty regularly over the last few months, organising the take-over and so forth. We've had some long interesting chats about you.'

'And?'

'Will you stop saying that! Your father tells me you've done a very creditable portrait of me.' He watched her closely.

'I had, but I destroyed it.' In a fit of temper! She had finally finished the portrait only to destroy it. She had been so depressed of late and the likeness of him staring at her day in and day out had been just too much to bear. It now stood in shreds in the corner of her studio, possibly her best effort to date, and all she had left of André.

He looked as if she had physically struck him. 'Why?' he asked dazedly.

She shrugged. 'I didn't want it any more.'

'I see.'

'Do you?' She hoped not; the last thing she wanted was for him to know she loved him. She didn't want to give him something else to taunt her with.

'I suppose so. You hate me—and I can't say I blame you after some of the things I've accused you of. But I want you to know the reason I treated you as I did, the reason I've taunted and abused you until you can't even bear to look at me. From the moment I first saw you I was deeply attracted. But I didn't want to be,' he added ruefully.

'You thought I was the maid,' she reminded him.

'And I thought you the most beautiful maid I'd ever seen. I wanted you, let's make no mistake about that. From the first I told you there was someone in my life, that someone was you. I wanted you very much. And then something happened that shook my world to it foundations.' He paused as if finding it difficult to carry on.

If Caroline didn't know better she would have said the cool, always self-assured André, was uncertain of himself. But that couldn't be possible, he was always confident, always sure. 'What happened?' she asked because it was expected of her, not because she cared to hear his answer.

'I fell in love with you,' he admitted simply.

His words were so quietly spoken that she couldn't be sure she had heard him correctly. 'Wh-what did you say?'

His eyes snapped with anger. 'I think you heard me, Caro.'

'But I—I don't believe you!' She turned away so that he shouldn't see the unshed tears shimmering in her eyes. 'This is just another way of tormenting me. What are you hoping for, a declaration of love on my part so that you can throw it back in my face? Because you won't get one, I can assure you of that!'

His face was twisted with emotion. 'God, you must really hate me if you can think that of me. But I don't care. You're attracted to me physically, and if that's all I can have from you then I'm prepared to accept that. I love you, Caro,' he said firmly, moving closer to her, the look in his eyes one of passionate intensity. 'I desperately want to make you my wife.'

'You want to marry me?' she squeaked, still not quite believing what he was saying.

He was so close now their bodies were touching. 'Want to marry you!' he groaned huskily. 'I think I shall go mad if I don't soon have you.' He bent his dark head to slowly caress her neck with his fevered lips.

'Surely you don't need to marry me for that?' She felt again that weakening of her limbs at his touch, felt his full arousal against her own body.

'Nothing less than the rest of my life with you will satisfy me. And I want you to have my children, I want that very much. But I don't want to talk any more, Caro, I just want to love you, to feel you close against me and your lips on mine.'

His actions closely followed his words and after a momentary holding back she felt herself melt against him in total abandon, her lips parting to receive the full onslaught to her already heightened senses. She fitted against him as if she had belonged there all her life—and she felt as if she had, that any life without André wasn't life at all but mere existence. Hadn't the last few months proved that!

He removed her jacket to move her back against the sofa, pushing her gently down into a prone position and quickly lying down beside her. His lips travelled passionately over her face, slowly down her throat, pushing aside the cream blouse to nuzzle against her bare breasts. His body was shaking in her arms.

'Oh God, oh *God*!' he groaned throatily, his skin moist with the effort it took him to control his longing to take her right now. 'I love you so much, Caro. You can't understand what that does to me. It makes me very vulnerable where you're concerned, and it's a vulnerability I've never welcomed into my life. But with you I find I don't care. Whether a marriage can work with love only on one side I have no idea, but I mean to give it a damn good try if you'll have me.' Those green eyes that could be sarcastically mocking gazed down at her pleadingly.

'André, I——'

His eyes darkened. 'Don't turn me down, Caro. I don't think I can take it. I'm completely at your mercy, and you could hurt me very badly. Please don't do that, darling. If you have to let me down, do it lightly.' Suddenly his face hardened, his skin almost grey in colour. 'But I won't let you go! If you turn me down I swear I'll follow you everywhere you go until you take pity on me and give in. Believe that!'

He really loved her! André, whom she had always believed to be above such things, was so much in love with her that his arrogant pride was no longer important to him. He wanted to marry her at any price, the least she could do was show him how much she loved him in return, that marriage wasn't important to her as long as he loved her.

Her eyes glowed as she looked up at him. 'I'm yours, André. You can take me now if you want me. You don't have to marry me, I'm all yours now.'

His eyes searched her face with disbelief. 'But you can't just offer yourself to me like this. I want to *marry* you!'

She smiled up at him in the darkness. 'And I'm telling you that you don't have to go to that extreme, that I'll come to you willingly without tying you to me for life.'

He shook his head. 'I want to be with you for life. Loving you means wanting you with me always, sharing and giving, and all that marriage entails. I'm not stupid, I realise we'll have a stormy time of it, we're both too stubborn for it to be any other way. But it's marriage or nothing,' he stated adamantly.

'Can't it be both?' she teased softly.

His brows drew together. 'Both?'

'Marriage and making love to me now.'

He shuddered in her arms, his hardened thighs pulsating against her. 'Do you mean that?'

Her gaze never flinched once under his intent look. 'I mean it. Oh, André, I love you. I love you so much that the last six months have been absolute hell for me, tortuous frustrating months when just one smile from you would have made me die of happiness. You can't imagine how I feel now, how much your love means to me.' Her voice shook with emotion.

It was as if a light had been lit behind those emerald eyes of his, and he heaved a tremulous sigh of exquisite relief. 'You really love me?' he asked uncertainly.

Her answer was to reach up and pull his head down so that their lips met in searing pleasure, she taking the initiative and parting his lips to deepen the kiss. After his first initial reaction André took over, his hands cupping her breasts, caressing them to full burgeoning life. At last he drew away from her, resting his damp forehead on her own, his hands unsteady as he ran them through his hair already ruffled from her fevered caresses, moving back to take possession of her bare breasts.

'Mine,' he murmured at last. 'All mine. We're going back to London tomorrow to apply for a licence,' he stated firmly. 'And in four days we'll be married.'

'Married . . .' she echoed glowingly.

'Yes,' he said, taking control in the old André manner, the manner she preferred him to adopt. 'And then we're returning here for a couple of weeks' secluded honeymoon before flying over to see your father. And this time we'll steer clear of the Wells farm. Do my plans meet with your approval?'

'Oh, yes,' she sighed happily.

'In the meantime I'm not letting you out of my sight, day or night. I want you with me every hour of the day. When we're married I'm never going away from you on business. If you happen to be unable to come with me, maybe producing one of the several children we shall undoubtedly have, then I'll stay home with you. I've learnt during the last few months that life without you isn't worth living.' He looked down at her slender body. 'How does it feel to know you hold my entire happiness in that delicious body of yours, in the love I never guessed you could ever feel towards me?'

'Do you believe me now about not trying to trick you into marriage?'

'I believe you. Matt put me right about a few things, including my slight on your morals. I realise I was just as much to blame for your deception as you were. I was an arrogant swine.'

Caroline laughed gently. As if he would ever be any different! But it didn't matter, she loved him, arrogance and all. 'And I was being that snooty little girl you accused me of being. I was conceited enough to believe I should be the one to teach you a lesson. I was being arrogant too.'

'Mm,' again his lips travelled the length of her throat. 'Marriage to you is definitely never going to be dull. It can't begin soon enough for me.'

'Or me.' Long days and endless nights spent in André's arms. She longed for the time.

'But as far as I'm concerned my taking care of you begins right now.' His eyes became mesmerised by her breasts. 'Do you mind?' his head lowered.

She responded to his caressing lips, gasping her pleasure. 'I don't mind at all. Oh, André, André ...'

Harlequin Presents...

The books that let you escape
into the wonderful world of romance!
Trips to exotic places...interesting
plots....meeting memorable people...
the excitement of love.... These are
integral parts of Harlequin Presents—
the heartwarming novels read by
women everywhere.

Many early issues are now available.
Choose from this great selection!

Choose from this list of Harlequin Presents editions

Relive a great romance...
Harlequin Presents 1980
Complete and mail this coupon today!

Harlequin Reader Service

In U.S.A.
MPO Box 707
Niagara Falls, N.Y. 14302

In Canada
649 Ontario St.
Stratford, Ontario, N5A 6W2

Please send me the following Harlequin Presents novels. I am enclosing my check or money order for $1.50 for each novel ordered, plus 59¢ to cover postage and handling.

☐ 165	☐ 175	☐ 184
☐ 166	☐ 176	☐ 185
☐ 168	☐ 177	☐ 186
☐ 169	☐ 178	☐ 187
☐ 170	☐ 179	☐ 188
☐ 172	☐ 181	☐ 189
☐ 173	☐ 182	☐ 190
☐ 174	☐ 183	☐ 191

Number of novels checked @ $1.50 each =	$	
N.Y. State residents add appropriate sales tax	$	
Postage and handling	$	.59
	TOTAL $	

I enclose _____
(Please send check or money order. We cannot be responsible for cash sent through the mail.)

NAME _____
(Please Print)

ADDRESS _____

CITY _____

STATE/PROV. _____

ZIP/POSTAL CODE _____

Offer expires June 30, 1980.   00456406000

What readers say about Harlequin Presents

"I feel as if I am in a different world every time I read a Harlequin."
A.T. * Detroit Michigan

"Harlequins have been my passport to the world. I have been many places without ever leaving my doorstep."
P.Z. Belvedere Illinois

"I like Harlequin books because they tell so much about other countries."
N.G. Rouyn, Quebec

"Your books offer a world of knowledge about places and people."
L.J. New Orleans, Louisiana

*Names available on request

Remember when a good love story made you feel like holding hands?

The wonder of love is timeless. Once discovered, love remains, despite the passage of time. Harlequin brings you stories of true love, about women the world over – women like you.

Harlequin Romances with the Harlequin magic...

Recapture the sparkle of first love...relive the joy of true romance...enjoy these stories of love today.

Six new novels every month – wherever paperbacks are sold.

Harlequin Omnibus

THREE love stories in **ONE** beautiful volume

The joys of being in love...
the wonder of romance...
the happiness that true love brings...

Now yours in the HARLEQUIN OMNIBUS
edition every month wherever
paperbacks are sold.